I Can Touch
the Bottom

I Can Touch the Bottom

Ms. Michel Moore
and
Marlon P.S. White

www.urbanbooks.net

Urban Books, LLC
97 N18th Street
Wyandanch, NY 11798

I Can Touch the Bottom

ISBN 13: 978-1-62286-996-1
ISBN 10: 1-62286-996-6

First Trade Paperback Printing July 2016
Printed in the United States of America

10 9 8 7 6 5 4 3 2 1

Distributed by Kensington Publishing Corp.
Submit Orders to:
Customer Service
400 Hahn Road
Westminster, MD 21157-4627
Phone: 1-800-733-3000
Fax: 1-800-659-2436

I Can Touch
the Bottom

by

Ms. Michel Moore
and
Marlon P.S. White

DEDICATION

12/28/15
LONG LIVE LOVE!

ACKNOWLEDGMENTS

Ms. Michel Moore—This journey is never easy to make; however, this time, I made the trip with my husband and coauthor, Marlon P.S. White. I thank him for his patience with me and continuing support. My mother, my daughter Author T. C. Littles, my family and friends, and, of course, the readers who've supported my endeavors since 2005, it's nothing but love! A special shout-out goes to Yolanda McCormick who holds me down at my spot, Hood Book Headquarters, every week. You're more than my homegirl; you're a blessing!

Marlon P.S. White—My wife, Ms. Michel Moore aka Michelle D. White, thank you for sticking by me and always having my back. We been doing this thing here since '99. To my parents, my children Mercedes White and DeVaughnta Dunlap, I always will love you all; unconditionally. My day 1 out here; Ty Toles, my brother, we can do anything we want in this world as long as we are thinking. You already know what it is. Kamel Mitchell, we both made it out of the belly of the beast. Salute. My family and especially all the nonbelievers, yup, yup; WIN! WIN! WIN! I WILL NOT LOSE! Of course, God, who never left my side even in my darkest moments, I pray you keep blessing me. And to Mr. Carl Weber, Chances Make Champions; thanks for the opportunity for me to make history—*YOUNG & HUNGRY*—Coming Soon!

CHAPTER ONE

Years up in that motherfucker; straight wasted. Caged up like some wild animal that's used to roaming the streets. Alienated from my people like a nigga had the plague or something. I swear, I hope the garbage-mouthed rats that sold me out rot in hell. You don't turn your back on a real one like me; we a dying breed, and that's on everything. Yup, hell, yeah, them bastards tried to hold me up. And yeah, they slowed me down, that ain't no lie. But fuck outta here. I'm back on the block in full swing on some O. G. shit. On top of my game where a guy supposed to be. Now if that ain't God blessing my hustle, then I don't know what the hell you call it. Stack was tipsy, feeling good as he turned up the sounds in his truck. For him, everything was lovely. He'd done his time in the penitentiary, and now it was time to live like a king; stress free. *Yeah, tonight was a good-ass night for me! Matter of fact, the entire day was off the chain. The streets was acting right with my money, and them dusty females at the club was acting like they never seen a dude as polished as me. Shit can't get no better. Now all I need to do is get my stomach off craps, and I'ma be all the way a hundred.*

Stunt profiling in the butter-soft leather seats of his truck, all was well with Stackz as he reminisced. Blasting the rhythmic sounds of jazz, the music flowed out of the custom-installed speakers. Each beat of the multiple instruments seemed to be felt deep in his muscular built bones. Content with life, his fingertips tapped on the side of the steering wheel. Off into his own world, the semiwasted young-style gangster with an old-school mentality wanted and needed something hot to put on his empty stomach. After throwing back several double shots of 1738 at Club A.F.S.C., short for another fucking strip club, he was about spent.

Fighting the beginning numbness of a slight headache, he felt the rumbling movements of his ribs trying to touch his spine. Realizing he couldn't fight the need for food to soak up some of the liquor in his system any longer, he knew he had to get right. Stackz finally turned the radio's volume down to focus. Slowing down, he hit his blinker and busted a quick U-turn. Knowing relief from hunger was only minutes away, he pulled up to a local favorite late-night spot. They served breakfast twenty-four-seven which always came in handy when the pancake and scrambled eggs with cheese munchies kicked in. Stackz and his close-knit crew were semiregulars at the greasy spoon. They often stumbled in there to get their grub on after clubbing or getting wasted. But this time was different. Stackz wasn't crewed up with his team of menacing cohorts. He was rolling solo.

Looking through the huge neon-lit window, he immediately took notice that the "hood" restaurant was unusually empty for that time of night; a perfect setting for the impossible to be made possible. Any and everything was subject to jump off after 2:00 a.m. in Detroit, and no one, not even the toughest gangster, was exempt from getting got if caught slipping. Being cautious, Stackz had second thoughts of even stopping at the hole-in-the-wall, yet his stomach growling once more made up his mind for him. Stackz wasn't scared of the crime-plagued city at all. Matter of fact, he felt the city oughta be scared of him. He'd just come home after serving time in prison and was still on parole. But that wasn't going to hinder him from being the man he was on the streets or handling business on a daily basis; legal or not. And on that note, Stackz reached over to the passenger seat, grabbing his pistol. After putting one up top, he placed it on his lap.

Fuck that ho, a motherfucker don't wanna act a fool tonight bullshit; a nigga straight hungry as hell. Chili fries with cheese is just what a brother need to get me back right, Stackz thought as he pulled to the side of the building.

Stackz put his vehicle in park. With no worries, he jumped out of the triple-black Jeep Commander, gun in hand. Like a hawk hunting for prey, his eyes searched the general area, being mindful of his surroundings. Tipsy not drunk, the trained street soldier was on high alert and on point. Pausing momentarily, he tucked the rubber-gripped .45-caliber thumper in his waistband, adjusting it. He was a hood sniper when it came to automatics, so the fact he had his "li'l act right" with him, he was all good. Pulling his shirt down in an attempt to conceal the illegal peacemaker, Stackz reassured his still-disgruntled stomach that satisfaction was shortly on the way.

Shutting the truck door, he hit the lock button on his keychain. Checking the lot once more, he headed toward the restaurant entrance. As he made his way past the window, Stackz took notice of the people inside; three guys who appeared to be silly and harmless and two young females. Listening to their laughter from the outside, he assumed they were here on the same buzzed mission he was: needing a greasy fix.

With confidence, Stackz pushed the glass door wide open, stepping inside. It was whatever. On some Martin Luther King shit, tonight, he was fearing no man. As if on cue, all the laughter he'd overheard while walking up abruptly ceased. It was as if Jesus had jumped off the cross or Tupac's ghost had appeared for a final farewell concert;

all eyez were on him. After a few brief seconds of uncomfortable silence, the three initially-perceived-to-be-harmless dudes took on the form of pure thirstiness. Although Stackz felt he was outnumbered when it came down to it, he knew he was good with the hardware and would put in work, if need be. Maybe it was the 1738 flowing through his bloodstream making him paranoid—and maybe not. But whatever the case, Stackz immediately felt like the trio of guys possibly had some bullshit brewing and put his game face on.

Making eye contact with both of the girls, Stackz had the ability to quickly study people's body language and act accordingly. It was a gift that his grandmother passed down to him; one he often used to his advantage. The lighter skinned one with all the weave appeared to be wild. Smacking on her gum, sucking her teeth, and talking loud, she was everything that Stackz didn't like in a woman. He might have been locked up for some years, but he knew she was out of order. Her clothes were too tight and definitely too revealing for his taste. Whoever she was, Stackz could tell she was trying too hard. Not wanting to stare at the group of people too much longer, he quickly glanced at the other female. Immediately with ease, he read something in the caramel-complexioned female's mannerisms that said she wasn't down with the clown antics her group was into. Stackz made a mental note that although she was cute in the face and had potential, she was dumb as hell for hanging with dudes that appeared to be bottom-feeders.

"Hello, there, can I help you?" the girl behind the security glass asked, pen in hand as he approached the counter.

"Umm, yeah, dear, let me get some chili fries with bacon, Swiss, and American cheese, along with fresh chopped onions," he calmly responded, still being aware of the eerie silence since he'd come inside the building.

"Will that complete your order?" she leaned closer to the bulletproof glass, getting a whiff of Stackz's cologne that had somehow floated through to the other side.

"Yeah, sweetheart. That's it," Stackz replied, taking his money out of his pocket. While waiting for the total, he stared down at her name tag which read Tangy. He thought he knew her but couldn't call it for sure. Although he and his boys were semilate-night regulars, the virtually unskilled cashiers working the graveyard shift changed like clockwork. Waiting for the female who seemed somewhat familiar to give him his total, it suddenly hit Stackz where he remembered her from. She was T. L. people; his young soldier who he'd raised from a youth. He ran with a lot of chicks, but this girl's cat-shaped eyes were what he remembered.

Tangy had run with Stackz's protégé a few summers back and easily knew who he was. As soon as he had walked through the door, her heart raced. Tangy hoped her hair was on point and wished she'd worn her good push-up bra. She always had a secret crush on Stackz, like most females from around the way, even if they were banging one of his boys. Stackz always dressed nice, stayed driving good, and most importantly, was rumored to have a big piece of meat between his legs he knew how to work. She wanted nothing more but for him to sit in the dining-room area and eat his food, but with the three stooges and their girls still tucked away in the corner of the restaurant acting a fool, Tangy knew that would never happen. She was disgusted, constantly giving them the side eye as she rang up Stackz's order.

No rookie to the streets, Stackz peeped her unease and body language. He felt like something was up and knew right then and there he should get ready.

"That will be $5.37, please, Stackz," she quietly announced, seductively licking her lips.

Like Stackz thought he knew who she was, the fact she called him by his street name confirmed he was right. Tangy did, in fact, used to run with T. L. Nevertheless, Stackz was used to females openly flirting with him so he paid her no mind, especially at this moment. Without hesitation, he pealed a twenty-dollar bill off his medium-size knot and slid it to her, insisting she kept the change. Just then, Stackz overheard the biggest of the three guys posted in the far corner try to go hard.

"Who in the fuck this pretty-ass nigga think he is! All fly guy and shit with his red Pelle on and rocking them overpriced Robin's Jeans. He must not know where the hell he's at. He gonna mess around and get all the shit ran, plus that truck he drove up in."

Stackz clearly wasn't moved by his hating punk-ass comment. He knew just where he was; in the heart of the city; the city that he got hella money in. Stackz had already killed the nigga with all the mouth and his homeboys eight different ways in his mind before he could blink twice. *Got me a few to go, I see. Any sign of fuckery and they people ain't gon' be able to sell enough fish dinners or raise enough money in a GoFundMe account to bury they asses quick enough.*

"Stackz, you heard that right?" Tangy asked on the sly.

"Yeah, baby girl," he grinned, winking his eye. "I know where I am; just where the fuck I wanna be." Casually, he turned, looking over his shoulder at the trio, especially the one with the big mouthpiece. "Listen up, you ho-ass nigga; this ain't what you want. This right here ain't what you looking for tonight; none of y'all. So fall back with them bitches and relax. Don't tempt me to show out."

Overly intoxicated, the three drunk wannabe thugs huddled together, obviously getting their courage up to attack. With ill intentions of going for bad, each kept looking over in Stackz's direction, hoping their intended target was just talking that ballsy shit to convince himself he wasn't about to get got.

Stackz had already sized the dudes up when he first stepped inside the restaurant and knew if and when the time came, he'd lay all they asses down; the two groupie skanks also, if need be. In Detroit, females were known for having "gangster moments" too. So fuck all that "I'm innocent and was just with him because" bullshit. In Stackz's eyes, everybody could bleed blood if they jumped into the murderous street arena; hoes included. Holding his own, like the O. G. he was, Stackz stood by the counter. With his phone in one hand and the other ready to whip out his .45 and go to work, he was hyped.

"Dang, why y'all always stay on some unnecessary crap?" one female remarked loud enough so Stackz would hopefully hear. What she was really doing was dry snitching on the always drunk, belligerent clowns she was sitting with. She'd been around them long enough from time to time to know they were seriously out of their league where this guy was concerned. The way he stood and carried himself, Ava knew dude was right; trouble with him was definitely not what they wanted. "Look, Leela, I'm ready to go right fucking now. Fuck this dumb shit! Y'all tripping!"

"Naw, Ava, slow down—chill; we good. You always acting like you too good to hang out with me and my friends," Leela smartly replied with a look of disdain.

"Yeah, and creeps like these right here is the reason why I don't fuck with your ass on the regular." She stood to her feet, leering over at the plotting haters with disgust.

"Creeps, huh?" Mickey had been called worse in his life so he let that little insult roll off his back like water but took offense to her trying to cause a scene. "Yo, Leela, shut your sister the fuck up," he urged in a hushed tone as to not be heard by their soon-to-be victim. "Calm her uppity-acting ass down; all loud and shit. She gon' spook dude before we even get a chance to run his pockets."

"Oh hell to the naw," Ava loudly clapped back at Mickey, not caring who heard her. "I'm out of this motherfucker for sure! I ain't into catching no cases or bodies for the next dummy; especially your thirsty-trapping ass. Y'all do y'all!"

"Dang, sis, hold up for a few," Leela cut her eyes. Reaching over in an attempt to grab her little sister by the arm as she tried heading toward the door, she knew things were about to get out of hand.

"Yeah, hater, listen to Mickey and your sister. We on to something big right now, so chill! You can break out when we done and not before."

"Fuck your bum ass," Ava instantaneously snapped on Devin, the biggest in size of his wannabe tough crew; the one with all the mouth Stackz had overheard. "You might run Leela's simpleminded self 'cause y'all fucking around, but you ain't running nothing this way. You can bet that much." Still protesting her readiness to leave and the fact she wanted no part of whatever they were on, she pulled away from her older sibling's grip.

Devin grew heated. He hated to be contradicted, and hated even more for Ava to talk down on him and his boys. She had a bad habit of behaving like her shit didn't stank and she wasn't born, raised, and still posted in the same part of the city as he was. He didn't want her hanging with them anyhow tonight, but in between Leela wanting female company and Mickey always hoping he could one day get on, here Ava was; going against the grain, as usual. "Look, girl, I swear on everything I love, I'm straight bulldogging and skull tapping that ass if your people blow this lick for me with that bad luck mouth of hers."

Leela wasn't gonna front and act as if Devin's wrath meant nothing. Those ass kickings she received at her man's hands leisurely were taking a toll on her body. With that in mind, she once again pleaded with Ava to stop bugging. Leela tried reasoning with her that it was just about to be another simple strong-arm robbery that was about to take place.

So she believed.

Stackz was no fool by a long shot. He knew his own pedigree in the grimy streets he ran in. Real gangsters move in silence. So he didn't say one word, because if it came down to it, he didn't mind being the suspect in the interrogation room on the next season of *The First 48 Hours.* Unbeknownst to the three drunken thugs, Stackz had firsthand experience with cold-blooded murder and had no problem whatsoever sending them on their way.

"Here you go. You have a good night and be safe out here," side eyeing the thirsty trio yet again, Tangy gave Stackz a brown paper bag containing his chili-cheese fries.

Sensing some sudden movements from behind, Stackz was fast and on his 360 spin. Having already grabbed his food with the left hand, he swiftly reached behind his back with the right. Whipping out his .45 upping it as he turned around, it was on. Game time. Meeting the big man Devin's mouth with the pistol, he stopped him dead in his tracks as he brought it crashing down into his dental. The steel barrel shattered a few of Devin's teeth and busted his lip. Stackz was now in his zone. He'd stepped over into the dark side. With a menacing look on his face that read *I'm about to catch a case on that ass,* his heart raced.

"Arrggh." Blood ran out of Devin's mouth, dripping all over his once winter-white shirt. Feeling as if he was done before he even got started, Devin held both hands up in the air like the Mike Brown protester with his eyes closed. Bracing himself for the worst that was evident to come, the other would-be robbers jumped up ready to come to his aid.

Stackz was stern in his demeanor and words, dropping his much-needed bag of fries to the ground. He wasn't with no games, and he made sure everyone understood that much, shoving the gun's barrel in Devin's mouth as hot piss flowed down the wankster's pants leg. "Yup, come on with it, and I'm gonna send this here fat nigga to the upper room first. Then I got sixteen more 'li'l friends' to make sure you lames catch up with this big pissy bitch before he reach Jesus' front door. So what in the fuck it's gonna be, fellas? We rocking out or what, 'cause my food getting cold?"

Rank and Mickey straight-away stopped. They stood perfectly still, taking in all what Stackz had just said. It was as if they were frozen in time. They both considered their fate if they took another step, as well as Devin's. Confused and concerned, they turned to each other, not knowing what move to make next. Stackz was not in the mood to play around as his stomach was still growling. Ready to put an end to this entire failed attempt of them playing at being gangsters, he helped them decide. Snatching his burner out of Devin's bloody mouth, he pointed it at the defeated voiceless duo. Motioning his peacemaker toward the booth where the females were still posted at, Rank and Mickey quickly got the idea and politely sat back down.

"Oh my God," Leela gasped on the verge of tears, seeing her meal ticket getting his ass handed to him.

"Okay, back to you, fat boy." Stackz turned his attention back to Devin, "Mister, I'm the winner of the ho-ass nigga of the night contest." Not done with showing these fools that if you play with fire you *will* get burnt, Stackz gripped up tightly on his gun. With brutal force and an overwhelming taste for violence, he smacked Devin across the top of his head with the butt of the pistol. An echo rang throughout the walls of the restaurant. Cracking Devin's skull, blood started to leak from an instant deep gash. He was dizzy. The room was starting to spin as smells of bacon, cheeseburgers, and chicken finger aromas filled his flaring nostrils. Stackz had proven his point just as he claimed he would. Tangling with him wasn't what Devin or his crew of cowardly misfits wanted. "Now, okay, motherfucker, you see what it really is and what's really good. So we done here tonight, or you wanna go a second round?"

Devin tried to stand strong but couldn't maintain his balance. His knees buckled as his heavy frame dropped to the ceramic floor. Speechless, Mickey and Rank were in shock. They had never seen their peoples so humiliated by the next manz. It was like Devin was nothing to Stackz but a small child being punished for speaking out of turn.

With their mouths wide open in disbelief and horror, Ava and Leela held each other tight. The different-as-night-and-day sisters stayed at each other's throats, but at this point, they were as one. What started off as a late-night run to the restaurant to grab a bite to eat and hang out had turned to them being terrified to move an inch. Motionless, afraid for their lives, the girls did what most females would do in that situation.

Cry.

Praying they would make it out of there alive, Ava searched Stackz's eyes for any small glimmer of mercy he was willing to grant them. In between hoping she and Leela would see daylight, Ava was secretly elated Devin and them had finally met their match. They had a bad habit of thinking the world owed them something so Mickey and Rank getting ordered to go sit in the corner like some punk bitches was priceless. And as for Devin's big-mouthed fat ass sprawled across the floor, mouth busted, drenched in his own piss, that was nothing short of Christmas, her birthday, and tax refund time all rolled into one. Ava wanted to do cartwheels across the restaurant and break out in a cheer celebrating Stackz, but the fact he was holding a gun on her and her sister thwarted that thought. As crazy as it seemed, Ava was turned on in a sexual way. She was mesmerized seeing this fine-ass mystery man in total beast mode. Her pussy ached and tingled with every word he spoke and movement he made; even when his rage was directed at her.

"Okay, you two silly, sour-faced broads, bust the fuck up; get the hell on before I change my mind," Stackz irately ordered, giving them the opportunity to leave unharmed.

The fact they had come with the plastic thugs meant nothing. This was not one of those all for one, one for all moments. This game would be played solo, if need be. Terrified Devin's fate could easily become theirs if they got too close to the man didn't stop them from taking Stackz up on his offer before he did actually change his mind. Hauling ass toward the door, Leela was surprisingly first in line. Rushing by Stackz, who was towering over a bloodied mouth and head Devin, Leela's body trembled with fear. Lying on the floor holding his open wound, Devin tried to slow down the loss of blood. While he begged for his life to be spared, Leela never once made eye contact with her so-called man. Instead, almost knocking Ava to the ground to get by, she pushed the double exit doors wide open. Fleeing into the parking lot, Leela disappeared into the darkness of the late night not looking back, with Ava trailing closely behind.

CHAPTER TWO

Tangy was all in. Stackz had just become her hero. Watching him regulate not one, but three thugs at the same time, he'd definitely be her new man crush Monday on Facebook. Just as Ava was feeling some sort of weird sexual tension seeing Stackz boss up, so was Tangy. Working the graveyard shift in the hood, Tangy had seen just about every type of crazy shit pop off and heard the unimaginable. But tonight was the icing on the cake of them all. The dude she'd been crushing on since the first time she'd seen him was full-blown flexing and making that shit seem easy. T. L.'s mentor was holding court on the wannabe thugs that'd been trash-talking and intimidating customers all night. The guy Stackz had laid out on the floor had called Tangy out her name repeatedly. He also had his girl threaten to beat her ass not more than twenty minutes prior. So in Tangy's eyes, it was like *fuck him*. He needed some act right in his pathetic life.

The foreign cook felt the exact same as Tangy. He didn't want any trouble so he kept his head down, working on peeling potatoes. To him, it was just another normal late night at work. Since he didn't have his green card yet, he wanted no one from any of the two sides to even look at him as if he was interested. Barely speaking English, he was there to cook food and go home to his wife and four small children. He saw nothing; knew nothing; and cared about nothing.

"All I wanted was some damn chili fries. Maybe swing by a freak bitch crib to get some pussy and head and call it a night. But, naw, y'all thirsty niggas wouldn't let that shit go down like that. That shit was too much like right. Y'all wanted to see what it was like to go toe to toe with a dude of my caliber. Y'all was looking for this heat, so now you got."

"Whoa, hold on, bro," Devin spoke out as the room continued to spin from the blow on the head he'd suffered.

"Naw, shut the fuck up! Ain't no 'hold on' or 'time-out.' This shit is all the way live, and it's gonna stay that way. And for the record, I ain't your bro," Stackz announced, enraged what a simple stop at the local late-night food spot had turned into.

Devin did as he was told. He knew he had no win with Stackz at the moment. Dropping his head with his hands up, as to say okay, whatever you say, he prayed he could get to his gun. He looked over at his homeboys with a look of shame on his face. He wished Mickey and Rank would've backed him up when he originally made his move on their intended victim. Maybe then, things would have flowed differently. The tables would definitely be turned. Stackz would be half dead on the black-and-white dirty tiled floor, begging for his life instead of him.

Realizing it was time to bring this situation to an end, Stackz had to break out. A born thinker, especially in chaotic bullshit such as this, he formulated his next move. With only one way out of the restaurant, he knew what he had to do. Staring down at Devin, he let him know that for every action, there was going to be a reaction; some reactions worse than others. With those words of hood wisdom being bestowed upon Devin, Stackz then kicked him directly in the face. Just to make sure he got his point across, he then callously stomped the side of Devin's already traumatized head. The crispy fresh wheat Tims he'd coped earlier in the day now had bright red splatters of blood not only on the toe area, but the sides as well. Taking in account the door was at least ten or so feet away, Stackz slowly inched his way to the exit. Keeping his eyes focused on Rank, Mickey, and Devin, he wasn't sure if the thus far cowardly trio had guns on them or not. Raised in the streets of Detroit, he cautiously treated the situation as if they did.

Just as Stackz was nearing the front door, Tangy came from behind the bulletproof glass. Stepping over Devin like the piece of nothing nigga he was, she smiled, handing Stackz another bag. "Here you go, bae, some fresh chili fries on the house."

Stackz happily accepted the fresh hot food, almost forgetting the reason he'd stopped in the first place. "Good looking out, girl," he winked, backing up slowly toward the doors. Watching his would-be attackers like a vicious pit bull ready to pounce in a dogfight, his finger stayed on the trigger. Finally arriving at the exit, Stackz placed his back against the door. Using his weight, he pushed it wide open. Gun his right hand, food in his left, in a quick movement, he tucked the brown paper bag food under his arm. With that now free hand, Stackz reached down in his pocket. Pulling out his keys, he pushed unlock on the multibutton pad. In one click, the driver's door of his Jeep Commander popped up. Safely in the parking lot, the victorious warrior momentary stood at the side of his truck. Looking back into the Coney Island, he saw a lot of movement.

Making sure they were well out of harm's way, Mickey and Rank ran over to their boy's side. Lying on the floor both severely beaten and bloody, Devin moaned out in pain. Bending down, they aided him to get on his feet.

"Dawg, come on, get up! Get up! Let's go get on his ass before he dip." Mickey was now brave hearted in words, gripping the big man's elbow as he stood. "I'm gon' kill that pretty-ass nigga. Look what he did to you."

Almost in tears, Devin desperately fought to catch his breath. Suffering from high blood pressure, the over-weight ruffian was already two or three cheeseburgers away from a heart attack or stroke. Stackz's rough house blows to his face and side of the head had him still dazed even after the fact. Being helped over to a nearby booth against the wall, Devin sat down, looking as if he was moments away from passing out. Barely having control of himself to sit upright, he told them to go handle Stackz as he slumped over on his side.

Mickey and Rank stood tall. They didn't have a choice if they wanted to save face and have any sort of dignity left. Finally revealing their weapons from underneath their shirts, each ran outside. With guns drawn, the pair sought Stackz out to deliver a little bit of payback for his disrespectful treatment of Devin. Revenge would soon be delivered in a deadly fashion. Easily finding him at his vehicle, Rank knew they had to act fast seeing Stackz already had one foot inside his whip with the rest of his body soon to follow. Raising both pistols, the calmness of the late-night, early-morning air was interrupted as shots rapidly rang out.

Round after round was recklessly let loose. One, two, three. Eight, ten, twelve. It seemed like the hail of gunfire would never let up.

"Fuck, naw," Stackz mumbled as bullets whizzed past him, rocking his Jeep.

Posted side by side, Mickey and Rank were going all-out commando-style. Close up enough to see the fruits of their ill intentioned labor, the menaces' courage increased, seeing the bullets rip through the truck's rear door and shatter the thick, tinted glass hatch.

"What up, doe, now?" Mickey shouted, directly hitting the driver's side mirror.

Rank then chimed in, promising the ultimate revenge while doing his own equal amount of damage to the washed and triple-waxed Commander, "Whack pussy-ass nigga, yous as good as dead! Dead as a motherfucker!" Squeezing the trigger of his .45-caliber automatic, Rank held his firearm sideways like you see hooligans do in a bad, low-budget hood movie.

Stackz was heated; beyond pissed. Never mind the fact bullets were zipping around his body barely missing him. Of course, he was mad they were shooting at him; that goes without saying. But he was even more so enraged because his ride, his baby, was being abused, taking in huge gaping holes left and right. Simple Street-olgy 101; the worst thing a player in the game can do is shoot up a nigga'z ride. Especially if he had money invested in it.

Stackz wasted no time snapping into defense mode. His fury reached a hundred in no time flat. Automatically diving all the way in the truck, he ducked down, taking cover. Tossing the damn bad luck food in the brown paper bag aimlessly inside the truck, he listened to the ear-popping sounds of round after round being let off. Crouched over, Stackz reached into the driver-side door compartment where a normal person would often keep meaningless bullshit. Thank God, Stackz's DNA dictated that he was far from normal. Retrieving an extra clip he kept fully loaded, ready, just in case for situations like this, he was ready to go to war.

Climbing over to the passenger seat, he quickly put the clip in the back pocket of his jeans. Pulling the handle out, he swung open the door. Staying low, he positioned himself behind the car door. Stackz peeked with caution from behind his makeshift barrier. He knew from firsthand experience, the longer he stayed in one position, he'd be more likely to be a sitting duck, and one, if not both, of the amateur marksmen may get lucky. As the bullets continued to rock his truck from side to side, gaping holes started to appear in the door he was behind.

These young boys want it . . . Well, they 'bout to feel me. 1, 2, 3, he counted to himself, then brazenly made a mad dash toward the rear of the vehicle, gun blazing. Once making it there, he started to return fire more deliberately aimed at Mickey and Rank. With the first volley of shots, he aimed high at their faces. Stackz's motto was if you kill the head, the body will surely follow. In a matter of a few brief seconds, Stackz introduced them to what it was like to do battle with a real-life gangster.

Mickey's courageously tough-guy stand was abruptly cut short. His upper body jerked back. Instantaneously, his shoulder cap exploded on impact from the .45-caliber slug Stackz sent his way. "I'm hit! I'm hit! I'm fucking shot," he agonized before being struck once more. This time, the force of the bullet spent him completely around. As he dropped to his knees and fell to the pavement, Mickey held his shoulder. Bleeding profusely from the two wounds, he crawled behind a huge green metal trash Dumpster located in the rear of the restaurant. Almost in shock, Mickey started to pray, begging God to spare his life.

Having no focus or discipline, Rank was blindly shooting at Stackz, hoping to hit his mark. The more rounds he let loose, the more he realized it was as if Stackz were superhuman. None of his bullets struck the polished player, even though he'd emptied his clip. Taking cover behind a car also parked in the lot, Rank was terrified, feeling some wetness in his head. Reaching his hand up, he brought it down to his face. Rank wanted to pass out. It was blood. Like his cohort Mickey, he'd been hit as well. Hearing footsteps, he braced himself, knowing death was near. Fortunately, he heard his boy Devin's voice yell out.

"Yo, nigga, you think you just gonna do me like that up in that motherfucker, and shit gonna be all sweet? Naw, dawg, shit ain't going down like that. You gonna pay, homeboy." Gun in hand, Devin stumbled out of the restaurant door in search of Stackz. As blood from his open head wound dripped down onto his face, he went on with his impromptu rant, vowing retribution. "Yo, Mickey, Rank; where y'all asses at? Posse up, niggas! Let's bury this bright-skin faggot!"

Turning his head for a split second to the right, Devin caught a quick glimpse of a terrified Mickey lying slumped over behind the Dumpster. Unfortunately, for bad-boy-to-the-end Devin, it was the last thing he'd ever see. One of Stackz's bullets ripped through Devin's neck. The next slug tore through his left ear, exiting the right side of his face. Devin's brains showered the already filthy glass of the window's restaurant. His body collapsed onto the pavement. His pistol fell out of his once-closed hand and slid across the asphalt.

An eerie silence filled the air. Stackz had counted the rounds each shooter probably had and realized unless they had an extra clip like him, they were out of ammo; hit; tapped out. Stackz hoped they had seen what just took place with their appeared-to-be leader and scattered out of Dodge. On parole, the eager-to-stay-free Stackz had no intentions whatsoever to wait and find out if his calculations were correct. He wasn't a fool. He knew it wouldn't be long before the Detroit police either crept up on the fresh murder scene or were dispatched there. Either/or, it was time for him to do what he was trying to do before aggressively interrupted by Devin, Mickey, and Rank; go home. If the two survivors turned out to be rats and told the cops what they knew or bossed up to be loyal to the game and wanted street justice remained to be seen in the days to follow. Stackz would have to deal with either play they made next.

He took in mind everything that had just popped off in slow motion. He didn't panic before, during, or now. This wasn't his first shoot-out with wannabe assholes who mistakenly believed they were about that life and the way he lived, Stackz surely knew it wasn't his last. Running down the list of things he had to do next in his head he took a deep breath. *#1 Get away from the scene as soon as possible. #2 Get rid of the murder tool after making sure his prints were clean. #3 Call T. L. or Gee for damage control,* and lastly, but most importantly, *#4 find out who these three clowns are and who their people are.* If their folk were in the game, or even dreamed about being in the game, they might have the notion of getting revenge. And if they did feel ballsy, then the body count would have to go up; no questions asked.

Searching the now-seemingly deserted parking lot with his eyes, Stackz wanted nothing more than to go over and spit in Devin's face but had watched enough episodes of *CSI* while locked up to know his DNA on the deceased would be like signing his own arrest warrant. Climbing up in his bullet-riddled truck, he prayed it would start. Once again, blessed by the hustle gods, it did. Gun still in one hand, he threw the metal warrior in reverse. Backing out of the lot like a normal person that'd just picked up their carryout, Stackz played his departure cool, seeing how his rear window was shot out.

Driving maybe a good few miles or so, he stumbled up on an abandoned gas station. Full of trash and other debris scattered about here and there, he pulled around to the back. Checking his surroundings for the possibility of late-night crackheads in search of their next blow or greed-driven scrappers who might be lurking, Stackz turned off his headlights. Without fear, he then got out of the truck with his favorite throwaway in tow. Once more, he looked around to see if anyone was out and about.

Seeing it was all clear, Stackz wiped the gun clean with not only a dirty rag but some Windex and tire cleaner as well.

As quietly as possible, he lifted the lid of the rusty industrial-size Dumpster. The big blue commercial monster was full beyond capacity with probably just about every discarded unwanted item from nearby residents and other businesses that didn't want to bother with proper disposal. Trying his best to not inhale the awful stench that leaped into his nostrils, Stackz spit twice. The way it smelled, a dead body might already be in it, so any other random person would definitely think twice about Dumpster diving and lucking up on discovering his gun. Stackz said his final good-byes to the pistol he'd been carrying since his release from prison and tossed it inside its new home. Using a stick, he then covered it up the best he could with the other rubbish. Casually, Stackz walked back to his whip as if he'd not just minutes earlier committed a murder and disposed of the weapon used to commit that felony. Starting the engine, he drove off.

Stackz did what was next on his list of things to do if he hoped to get away with murder: get ready to call T. L., his always-on-point cleanup man. Extremely loyal and trustworthy, Stackz knew he could count on his young dog. He was a soldier in the true sense of the word. Stackz been feeding and grooming T. L. since he was nine years old and his mama was out there getting high, addicted to crack, heroin, and popping pills. T. L. saw a lot growing up and had been through shit no kid should have to. Stackz and his little brother had stepped up and practically raised T. L. Stackz and Gee used to trap out of his mama's crib. When they saw the conditions he was subjected to, the two of them took him into their own home, treating him like a son, making sure he went to the best school, buying him everything a normal kid should have, and should have kept him doing right, but the streets were embedded in T. L.'s DNA. Having everything still couldn't quench the thirst for the street life out of him. So they kept "their son" close to them every day, teaching him so he'd learn how to think like a gangster and move like a boss.

They could count on him to get whatever task at hand done; quickly and efficiently. Still haunted by his mother throwing him away like garbage, T. L. was resentful at times and a known hothead when need be. However, he looked upon Stackz and Gee like the father figures he never had; he was their family. And he was willing to do anything to protect his kin; blood or not.

Now, T. L. was loved by many and feared by the shady-ass seedy side of Detroit just like Stackz wanted and needed a true hood warrior to be. T. L. could put in work and clean up the dirt he or Gee couldn't touch.

With one hand on the steering wheel, the other hand held his cell. Pushing the button on the side, he used the voice command to call T. L. In a matter of seconds, it connected the lines. The phone began to ring as Stackz caught a night air chill from the draft of not having a rear window. Looking over at his radio, Stackz saw the clock on the face read a little bit after three forty-five. Yet, it didn't matter how early or late it was. T. L. was on call twenty-four-seven always ready for action; good to go. For him, if it meant going to full-blown war at daybreak, he'd be as wide awake as if it was four in the evening.

On the second ring, T. L. answered. "Big bro, what up doe with you?"

"Yo, fam, what it do? I need you on deck ASAP on some real type of no-way-back-from-the-darkness business." Stackz seethed, still angry the three clowns had forced his hand into murder, even though it was self-defense.

T. L. was at his crib laid up with one of his many FFs, short for fuck friends. He grabbed the remote control to the flat-screen television and pressed mute. Having heard Stackz say "no way back from the darkness," T. L. sat straight up. He knew that was code name for someone had just got sent on their way. Intensely listening to his mentor run the evening down almost blow by blow, the eager-to-please goon got heated. Remembering he wasn't alone, he got out of bed with ole girl, not really knowing who she knew or could've been related to. She could be playing like she was asleep while ear hustling on the sly.

T. L. understood Detroit was the smallest big city ever, and if a nigga was trying to hide his black ass after doing dirt, unless you were as careful as him, Stackz, and Gee, that feat would be damn near impossible. Gathering his clothes, he got dressed while still listening to Stackz's game plan. "Yeah go ahead, bro. I'm on you. I'm throwing my shit on now and half out the door on my way." T. L. left the sleeping female in his bed, knowing she knew better than to touch a damn thing in his crib and risk getting her head knocked clear off her body.

"Okay, dig this here. I need you to shoot over to the spot where we always grab the food from."

"The spot with the food?" T. L. questioned, wanting to get the facts right.

"Yeah, the spot over from around the way," Stackz reaffirmed as he slowed down at a red light. "You know, where we hit up at when we come from the club. I had to turn up on these fucking clowns. I guess they was bugging and was sleep on a nigga thinking I was some sort of come up."

"Word?" T. L. quizzed, grabbing his car keys off the table.

"Yeah, your homegirl a cashier now up in that mother-fucker. Taking orders and shit."

"Who you talking about?"

"You know, what's her name? The honey with them funny cat eyes. The one you used to run with from the East Side. I saw her name tag, but that shit done slipped my mind."

From the description Stackz was giving, T. L. easily now knew who he meant. "Oh yeah, Tangy."

"Yeah, yeah, that's her," Stackz replied, nodding his head. "She saw the whole play go down; her and the damn cook."

"Word?"

"Yeah, my dude. So you already know I need that surveillances footage. I can't risk making the news on some murder shit. You know I get banged on any more felonies, my ass is straight cooked."

"Naw, naw, say no more, bro-bro. I got this! I'm on it right now! I'm on my way out the door and en route as we speak." T. L. jumped in his car as his adrenalin pumped. "The way the police move in Detroit, I can beat them there and swoop up that tape."

Stackz knew he could count on his young dawg to handle things. "Good looking out."

"Come on now, fam, it ain't no thang. You know how we do. So I'll hit you back when I'm good with it."

"The way she was playing it with me, I think she up for helping us out. She seem street as hell."

T. L. laughed, knowing Stackz had hit the nail on the head. Tangy was street as hell; a little *too* street for him. That's why he stopped messing with her. She wanted to mean mug and skull drag every other female he knew. "She definitely about her coins, so I got a couple racks on me to ensure I don't hear 'I can't,' 'no,' or 'I'm scared' shit fly outta her mouth. You feel me? Money talks and potential cases get bought."

Stackz had one reply equally as clever and true as T. L.'s statement. "You already know real ones buy what they want, what they need, and what they please. Right about now, I needs that surveillance footage."

CHAPTER THREE

Ava couldn't believe what had just taken place. She was pissed, not only at her sister for dragging her out of the house tonight to hang with Devin and his whack-minded cohorts, but herself for being so stupid to agree to come. She knew Leela's MO when it came to being in the middle of drama. It was like she craved that bullshit and found a way to find it, even if it wasn't looking for her. Now just like that, here they were on foot, in sandals, no less, running down a no-streetlight-deserted block, trying to make it to their mother's house.

"What the fuck be wrong with you?" Ava barked, glancing back over her shoulder while keeping it moving.

"Huh?"

"I said what in the fuck is wrong with you? Why you always down with this dumb shit? I can't believe you sometimes."

"What? Huh?" Leela once more replied, trying to keep up with her obviously angry sibling.

Ava wasn't having her older sister play the dumb role; not now; not tonight. "Listen, don't *huh* me, bitch! You know good and damn well what the fuck I'm talking about. You seen how that oversized sloppy animal you be running around with tried to attack that dude. Him, Mickey, and Rank always tripping."

"Okay and . . ."

Ava was infuriated with her big sister as well as almost out of breath but still kept it a hundred. "Okay, and he was minding his own business trying to place his order and *bam!* I guess that was too much like right to Devin and them, huh? Both of y'all dumb asses deserve each other. I swear to God I'm done with you!"

"Whoa, why you care so much about some random-ass buster? You must've been feeling ole boy or something, even though he called himself going on us." Leela dialed Devin's number but got no response.

"Leela, please stop being so damn stupid all the time. I ain't feeling nothing except for doing the right thing before karma comes around calling. You think that shit a joke, but it ain't. Karma will mess the fuck around and skip over your dumb ass and latch ahold of your kids."

"Yeah, whatever; man, fuck karma," Leela arrogantly giggled while running by a yard full of thick overgrown bushes, cell still in hand. "Karma don't want shit messing around with me or my badass, good-begging kids!"

Ava was outdone that her sister, a mother herself, had such little regard for doing the right thing when need be. She hoped her nieces and nephew would not turn out like the rest of the bloodline in their shady family tree: ruthless, rotten, and worthless. "Look, girl. Like I said, I'm over you and your no-good friends. The next time you wanna ask me to hang with Devin, Mickey, and Rank, don't—because the answer is going to be naw. Matter of fact, *hell naw!*"

Leela wanted to stop dead in her tracks and curse her little sister out for going so hard, but the darkness of the night changed her mind. She wisely decided to just keep it moving and deal with Ava and her opinions when they reached their destination. Hopefully, their mother would not be drunk and passed out and they could get in. Two blocks later and creeping through the vacant lot, the sisters were soon in the backyard of their childhood home. Seeing the blue light from the television peek through the tattered shades of the back bedroom, Ava exhaled as Leela reached up, tapping on the window. After what seemed like a lifetime, they finally heard a voice mumbling. Seconds later, they were met with their mother's bloodshot eyes peering at theirs.

"Why you two ungrateful bitches over here bothering me, waking me up? Y'all got y'all own damn house," she slurred as the flimsy door flung open. "Well, at least, Ava wannabe uppity ass do!"

"We know, Mom, but it was an emergency," Leela blurted out as she brushed past her mother's shoulder, barging inside. "Where my kids at? What they been doing?"

"Emergency, my ass! Ava, why you ain't just used the damn spare key I gave your butt!" Standing in the doorway, Leela's mother was almost snatched out of her drunken state of mind hearing her oldest child act so dense. "And as for you! Listen, you silly tramp. You know good and damn well them babies is sleep this time of morning, just like you and old wannabe white over there should be. But, naw, y'all disrespectful asses all up over here in my shit knocking on back windows and asking dumb shit."

Once both girls were inside the dimly lit dwelling, their mother finally stopped running off at the mouth and stumbled back to her bed to continue to sleep off the half pint of cheap wine she'd gulped down before passing out. As if on cue, the sibling arguing resumed.

Ava wasn't against her sister; she just had officially grown tired of backing up all her stupid plays. She was done with agreeing with the chaos she brought, not only into her own life but into the lives of everyone she'd come in contact with; not excluding her own children. Leela had a bad habit of not wanting to pay her rent wherever she lived, ultimately resulting in her and her babies to get put out, leaving Ava and their barely functioning alcoholic mother to step in and pick up the slack. This time was no different than the others; the kids were staying with their grandmother, while Ava was allowing Leela to temporarily stay in the converted dwelling home she'd bought in a county auction late last summer. But the unfit mother that lived to keep up bullshit and bring unwanted drama to her sister's home had just about worn out her welcome.

"Leela, please just tell me why you insist on hanging with those dirtballs? They always off into some devious shit; especially Devin. If he wouldn't been trying to start shit with that man . . ."

Examining the broken strap on her sandals, Leela casually glanced up, shaking her head like her sister was speaking in some sort of foreign language. "I'm sorry, but are you still talking to me? I already done told you forget that nigga you so worried about! Was you not just there in that motherfucker when he was pointing a gun at our black asses, calling us sour! You see how he had Devin; talking to him like he was crazy!"

Ava shook her head. Leela was everything she was not. Even though their mother claimed they had the same father, Ava wasn't so sure if that was the truth. Leela had to be the spawn of Satan. No matter what the younger sister said or tried, Leela was not in the business of listening. Instead, she continued to boast and brag about Devin and the many times he'd blessed her with money from his small-time hustles and capers. The fact that Devin and his boys oftentimes fucked over innocent people to get that "come up" Leela seemed to think was as great as, if not better than, winning the Powerball, meant nothing.

"Have you lost your damn mind? You sitting over here talking about Devin like he some sort of person that needs an award or something. That boy ain't nothing but a small-time, nickel-and-dime hustling thug. Him and Mickey and Rank out here always trying to go for bad."

"And . . ."

"And that's why that dude got him and them at gunpoint. Shit, matter of fact, they probably halfway to jail by now, so . . ."

Leela paused protesting Ava's statement as she whipped back out her cell to once again call. "Girl, you sound like a fool. Devin is that real deal. Trust me, I done seen him turn the tables and walk the fuck away from shit way worse than that. He gonna bless me big time off the pockets of that pretty boy nigga you seemed so worried about."

Yeah, we'll see. Ava sat back gathering her thoughts while watching her naïve sister live in a fantasy.

CHAPTER FOUR

Tangy eased her way toward the rear of the building and into the back office. The door squeaked loudly as she pushed it opened, stepping inside, but since she and the cook were the only ones working, it didn't matter. Like he'd ignore the uproar in the dining area, he didn't care what Tangy did either. The sign hanging on the door which read Managers Only in bold letters meant nothing to the ghetto princess-in-training. She was on a mission and was not going to allow a piece of paper with a hand-written order hinder her task. There were stacks and stacks of old receipts for food and dairy products, a small apartment-size refrigerator the owner kept his special meals in, and, of course, a desktop computer attached to several monitors. Having had several attempted robberies in the past, the Middle Eastern-descent owner was required by his insurance company to have them installed.

Peeking back out the door before heading to handle her business, Tangy saw the coast was clear. Closing it back as quietly as she could, she raced over to the computer. Looking up at the monitors, Tangy saw the parking lot in clear view. Not having to wonder about all the commotion that was going on, she knew it was one of the assholes that tried to go for bad with Stackz laid out. She and the cook were smart enough to duck and take cover when they heard the thunderous sound of the barrage of bullets ric-ochet off the building. Sure, the owner said the glass they were working behind could withstand the force of bullets; however, they were smart enough not to take the chance to see. No way did they want to run the risk of being struck by a stray bullet, so they made sure to stay put until they knew it had ceased.

Tangy looked for the eject button for the USB flash drive storage. Finding it, she then pressed the button, stuck it in her pocket, and smiled. Hitting a few more keys, she pulled up the recorded footage of Stackz giving the three clowns the business inside and outside of the restaurant. Watching Mickey get hit, then Rank followed Devin, taking a gunshot to the side of his head, Tangy knew the heinous, but valuable-to-some video had to go. Delete, Delete, Delete, she pressed with a smile on her face. After deleting the footage in every place she could think of in the system, Tangy was mindful to empty the recycle bin. Trying to bring the deadly events up again, she was content knowing she'd successfully erased all traces of the lethal altercation.

Opening the desk drawer, she rambled through it until she found one of the unmarked flash drives to replace the one she had just taken out. Pleased with herself, she wiped the computer down with an old, dirty-looking, grease-filled rag the day shift manager kept hanging in the office. She also wiped anything else she thought she may have touched. Before leaving, Tangy opened a bottle of water that was amongst many stored by the side of the door. To give herself extra insurance that the system would be tripping, she poured water across the keyboard and directly into the back of the computer. Leaving the bottle tipped over on the system as if the midnight manager had accidentally spilled it, Tangy exited the office.

Swiftly returning to the front, she cautiously came from behind the bulletproof glass. Glad that no more customers had come in, she had time to creep over to the window. Turning up her nose at what used to be a part of Devin's brains sliding down the window, she could only shake her head how Stackz had flipped the script on not one, but three dummies who wanted to go for bad.

"Yo, Sam. Go make some hot bleach water so you can mop up this crap," Tangy yelled back over her shoulder. Taking a quick survey, she saw a motionless Devin sprawled out near the doorway, Mickey still hiding by the Dumpster, as well as Rank, wide-eyed, seemingly in shock. Tangy knew the police would be coming at any time now because an injured Mickey was yelling into his cell phone for help; no doubt, 911. Unlike Devin, who at least went out like a real street player, and Rank, who couldn't manage to speak, believing the head wound he was suffering from was far worse than it truly was, Mickey was crying like a real little pussy. Tangy knew right then and there Rank might boss up and handle shit in the streets. Mickey, on the other hand, would be the weak link when it came down to it; code name: snitch bitch.

T. L. turned his kitted Charger up into the restaurant parking lot. Smooth enough to have never been caught up or directly linked with any of the drama he'd brought to residents of Metro Detroit and the surrounding areas, T. L. had his CPL. Carrying his firearm, legal or not, T. L. was like Stackz and Gee; he feared no man. So rolling down his window, T. L. had no problem worrying who might have been lurking, attempting to try him like they had his manz, or even the police showing up, wanting to frisk him for just being black. He was ready and legal for whatever. Surveying the scene, he couldn't help but to be elated at his fam's handiwork.

Damn, my guy, this is how you leave a buster and put that shit down! Laid flat the fuck out leaking from the head. Ho-ass bitches can't fade a real gangster rocking out from our set; impossible.

T. L. could clearly see inside the restaurant through the huge, and what appeared to be, blood-splattered window. His homegirl Tangy stood behind the counter casually filing her fingernails as if her workplace was not a bloody mess and the slow-moving response time, short-staffed cops were not on their way. As if she sensed him outside, Tangy looked up from what she was doing and easily recognized T. L.'s car. With a quickness, she perked up, fixing her hair and knocking off any crumbs that were possibly on her T-shirt and apron.

Unlocking the otherwise secured door once more, Tangy then headed back out in the dining area. Careful not to step on the mess on the floor she was about to have the cook mop up, she yelled to her coworker, "I'll be right back! And dang, yo, come clean this bullshit up before the police come they asses in here asking us all types of unnecessary garbage about shit you or me don't wanna be a part of."

Exiting the dining area in a hurry, Tangy ran outside. Stepping over Devin as if he wasn't even there, head held high, she grinned, thinking it's all fun and games with these lames until a real-life gangster falls through and up that gun.

T. L. was smooth as always. Licking his lips, he smoked Tangy over as she slow strolled, approaching his ride.

Crazy as ever, she was, of course, all smiles, acting as if she hadn't just stepped over a dead body in the middle of the parking lot. "Man, where you been hiding at? I tried to get at you, but I ain't got your number. You change that mug every few minutes."

T. L. didn't know what her nonchalant deal was where the slumped body was concerned and didn't have time to investigate. He had to get what he came to get and get the hell out of Dodge. "Girl, you know what it is. I'm out of here in these streets. You either keep up or catch up with a nigga; you feel me? But on another note, I need you to do me a solid."

Tangy stared him directly in the eyes with her hands planted firmly on her hips. "Tell me I got the best pussy in the world."

"Huh? Say *what*, now?" T. L. was completely thrown off by her wild and out-of-the-blue question.

"You heard me. I said, tell me I was the best pussy you ever had in life. Tell me I'm the shit!"

Once again, T. L. had a flashback to why he stopped fooling with her. Tangy was a 100 percent plum Negro nuts. Knowing he had to play her game to ensure he could quickly get what he needed from her, he did just that. "Come on now, Tangy, you know how we used to do what we do when we did what we did." He reached his arm outside of his car, tugging at the upper rim of her leggings, bringing her body toward him. "Now, seriously, I need you to hurry up and do something for me."

"Hey, love, I'm already on it." Seductively, she pulled out the flash drive of the made-for-TV shootout from her bra. Making sure T. L. got a good look at her double Ds, she leaned over inside the vehicle.

Not blind, he definitely got a good long look as he licked his lips, mimicking LL Cool J. Feeling a hard-on developing, he grabbed down at his dick. "Damn, baby, you a rider, for real!"

Tangy, not only crazy but a true freak to her heart, immediately got a glimpse of his bulging dick and wanted to taste it once more, just for old time's sake. "Listen, love, you know I always got your best interest at heart.

I knew when I seen your people come in the restaurant, it was gonna be my lucky night. I got to finally catch up with your big dick having ass. So, what's up for when a bitch get off? We fucking or what? What's the deal?"

Taking the flash drive out her hand, he had to laugh as he spoke. "You see, that's why I fucks with you! You a real stand-up bitch! Down for whatever, and a nigga ain't gotta tell you what to do or how to do it. You stay on point."

"Yeah, fuck them busters! They had that shit coming. Especially fat boy lying over there with all the mouth! Coming all out here like he superbad! He should of just stay down when he got laid down; dummy!"

T. L. licked his lips once more. "Damn, I dig your gangster ass! You keeps it real, fo'sho!"

"Okay, *that's* what I'm talking about, daddy. So what you got for me? When I'm getting some more of that hard pipe you be laying down?"

T. L. saw that Tangy was being relentless about them hooking up again and didn't wanna run the risk of offending her before the cops got there and she scornfully ratted Stackz out. "Dig this, my baby. I got something for you better than this dick!"

"Better than your dick, nigga? What in the entire world could be better than your dick?" She stood up, shifting all her weight on her right hip.

T. L. was appreciative of the compliment paid to his python, and under any other normal circumstances, he might have broken Tangy off some dick, but here and now, he had to be out and meet up with Stackz. "You right, ain't shit better than this motherfucker right here, but this might come in a close second." Reaching under his seat, T. L. pulled out a small wad of cash wrapped in red and beige-colored rubber bands. "Here, this is for you. A little something something for being my rider and having my people's back."

Tangy practically snatched the dough out of his hands before he could change his mind. "For real, for me?"

"Yeah; for you. And, hey, make sure dude good in there too that's moping. I know he needs to be looked out for."

"Don't worry about him, love. I'll take care of him personally, even if I got to throw him some of this cheese or put this fat pussy on his face."

T. L. peered through the restaurant window and turned his attitude back on grim. "Okay, now, bae! 'Cause you know, I don't mind putting that motherfucking sand nigga's ten toes up."

"Boy, you know, I know, you don't give two rotten shits about putting work. I ain't just meet your crazy ass. That's why we need to be together!"

"Aye, girl, before I bounce, put my number in your phone."

Smiling hard, Tangy quickly pulled out her MetroPCS from her back pocket. Making sure she wasn't making any mistakes, she then began punching the digits in her cell as T. L. called off his number. He told her to call him and keep him posted on any developments. Hearing sirens off in the far distance, Tangy knew them boys were on their way and stepped back away from T. L.'s whip as he put it in gear to pull off. Driving by the building, he looked over at the mayhem left behind by Stackz one more time.

"Amped up!" he said with certainty as he reached for his cell. "Now *that's* how you leave lames; that's on some ho shit," he laughed out loud hitting the gas, skirting out of the parking lot and onto the main road.

As T. L. sped through the dark, burned-out, once-vibrant city blocks of Detroit, he held his cell phone in one hand. Hitting speed dial, Stackz's cell phone was connecting to his. On the third ring he answered.

"Speak! Like only bosses can do."

T. L. spoke one word. "Done!"

"You got it? We good?" Stackz anxiously inquired.

"No doubt, I got it," T. L. confidently replied proud of himself for handling what was needed of him. "I got the footage and dig this! Homegirl lifted the shit and deleted all traces of that minidisaster you laid down. She put another drive in to cover her tracks. Nigga, you a straight ghost!"

"Oh yeah," Stackz nodded, glad it had worked out in his favor.

"Plus, I gave her a few of them big faces. Bitch said if the cook doesn't play right she'll dead his ass herself, personally. I even told her to keep me updated. So you good, bro-bro. I ain't never gonna let down the hand that blessed me."

T. L. loved to hear the O.G. spit that boss shit. It made him feel like their entire crew was untouchable. "In real life, fam, that's real talk. Blood in, blood out; you know how we do. Say no more. Well, keep that in a safe place, and we'll meet up tomorrow. I straight appreciate you, T."

"Well, hit me up later when you get situated. And be careful out here in these Detroit streets, boss. You already know these thirsty niggas on the come up don't give a fuck about nobody."

"No doubt." Stackz hated he was riding without his favorite pistol, but knew he had to leave it where he did. "But you best believe I'm about to handle a few more things and call it a night."

"All right then, Stackz, I'm about to pull up at my crib. A nigga left one of my hoes up in my shit playing like she was sleep. And you know how nosey bitches get when they by themselves too long in a dude's spot; they get to rambling; playing detective and shit."

"Hell, yeah, I already know how these jump offs get down," Stackz laughed, agreeing with his boy.

"Little momma fine as hell, but I'd hate to have to put a plastic bag over her fucking head."

He and Stackz laughed hard because they had no issues with killing nosey bitches. After gathering themselves from their good laugh, they both said "one," then disconnected the phone line.

CHAPTER FIVE

After hanging up his phone from talking to T. L., Stackz jumped onto the expressway. Dialing a number he had memorized in his head, he knew what had to come next in his plan to stay prison free. It was in the early hours of the a.m., but, the Detroit underworld never slept. Just like he knew the guy he was calling never slept and would answer by the second ring.

"Yeah, who dis?"

"Me, nigga; Stackz!"

"Oh, okay. What's good, fam? What's the deal?"

"A whole lot right now. I need to come through like ASAP. So I'm about to pull up on you in about ten or fifteen minutes tops."

"Come on. We working now. You know our doors open twenty-four-seven. Only time they're not held up in this sweatbox motherfucker is when them boys turn the heat up on this side of the city. Then we go dark."

Switching from the middle lane to the right-hand lane to exit the expressway, Stackz slowed his bullet-riddled Jeep down. There wasn't much going on at 4:45 in the morning, other than the normal crackheads shuffling about, lurking to come up on whatever change they could to get their next rock, so navigating to his destination was easy. Stackz just wanted to avoid any contact with the police, knowing there was no way in hell he could explain his window being shot out or the many slugs that were probably now housed in the body of his vehicle.

Stackz made a right on Canton Street and the boulevard. He was now in the heart of the Old Historic Packer District that once fed the city's hardworking people that were trying to make a living. Filled with abandoned houses, vacant lots, and dead bodies found in the run-down empty warehouses, no regular person not doing dirt ventured that way. Finally reaching his destination, a warehouse that used to be a semitruck repair shop, Stackz pulled up and cut his lights. Inching his shot up Jeep Commander in front of the laser sensor garage door big enough for eighteen-wheelers to drive through, he sighed in relief he'd made it clear across town, police-contact free. Looking up at a small, inconspicuous camera located on the high upper side of the graffiti-covered building, Stackz stuck his head out the window, throwing his hands up.

Inside the well lit warehouse, a skinny, dark skinned mouse of a man was preoccupied grubbing on a leftover piece of Popeye's he'd just warmed up. Seeing the red light blink on and off twice, he knew it was business on the floor. Pushing himself away from his any-and-everything-covered desk, he tossed the half-eaten drumstick on a stack of old newspapers. Standing up, he walked over to a shelf that held a nice-size colored security monitor. Getting a closer look at the image, a sense of urgency came over him as he recognized Stackz. Reaching down on his thick leather belt, he grabbed hold of the two-way walkie-talkie on his hip he ruled his lucrative illegal kingdom with.

"Hey, open up the main door. Let my people in and hurry up," he ordered, heading toward the main area of the building.

***

Stackz put his head back inside of his whip. As the huge door began to slowly move upward, he put his truck back in gear. All he saw at first were lights and legs, inch by inch. One would never know a major chop shop was operating inside unless he or she was plugged into Detroit's criminal underworld like Stackz, of course, was. Careful not to run over any of the many guys that were running around doing this and that, he steered in with ease.

A dingy, light skinned mechanic directed him in like an airport traffic controller on the clock. "Come on, come on. That's it; you gotta pull it up right here."

Stackz thought to himself Derrick had come a long way from his mama's garage chopping up cars, tagging them, getting petty money. Now he was dealing in the major league. From what Stackz could tell, there was at least a team of fifteen men that were taking parts off the vehicles and removing serial numbers or had blowtorches in hand. Stackz looked back over his shoulder at his Jeep and got prepared to say his final good-byes.

Out of the corner of his eye, he saw his homeboy coming down a set of stairs that he knew led from the upper office. Stackz walked toward his childhood friend that also had a baby by his first cousin. When Stackz reached Derrick, the pair gave each other some dap.

"Yeah, what'sup, my nigga, Pissy," Stackz mocked, calling Derrick by his nickname the kids had cruelly given him growing up. The now headman in the city making vehicles go *poof* never wanted to stop playing outside as a child and go use the bathroom, thinking he would miss out on the fun. So while they all played, Derrick would piss on himself, as if the other kids couldn't smell him.

"Yo, guy, don't be calling me fucking Pissy! That shit was so damn long ago." Derrick muffled his voice as he looked around the chop shop feeling embarrassed.

"So you say, Pissy. My cousin told me you still used to pee in the bed when y'all was still fucking around."

Derrick laughed, acting as if he was gonna swing on Stackz. "Whatever, guy, but on the real . . ." He headed toward the Jeep that had extremely visible bullet holes throughout the body. "What's the deal, fam; who the fuck tried to take your ass out of the game? This shit's crazy." He stuck his finger in a few holes, surveying the damage.

"Look, guy, I need this truck to disappear off the face of the earth like magic. I need you to do some old 1, 2, 3, David Copperfield on this bitch. Make it ghost, you feel me?"

"Yeah, dawg, ain't no thang. I'm on you. I can do that, no problem." Derrick rubbed his hands together, seeing nothing but more money on the near horizon.

Stackz saw the greedy gleam in Derrick's face and wasted no time setting him straight on what exactly had to be done. "Look here, motherfucker, I see them damn money signs dancing in them ugly eyes, and I ain't trying to entertain the bullshit. Now, I need this bitch ghost for real. Not no black market tagging, transplant situation. That's *not* what needs to pop off," he demanded as he walked up, evading Derrick's personal space to make sure he clearly understood the words that were coming out of his mouth. "I need this Jeep gone; *gone*. All the way melted down, rebirthed into some fancy overpriced bedrails on sale on the West Coast; you feel me? Gone! Now, what's really good?"

Damn, this a gang of money he want me to just throw away. Shaking his head, Derrick was more than disappointed none of the highly sought-after parts could at least be harvested and resold for cash. He hadn't grown so big in the chop shop not going beyond the call of duty. He'd resale, retag, or double sell his own mother's ride if he thought there was a slight profit in it. "Oh, you want the total breakdown. Well, you know it's gonna be a ticket on that."

"And what, nigga? What's your damn point? I know you ain't playing me like I'm light in the pockets or something, is you? 'Cause you know that ain't never ever been the case! Don't act like you don't know me and how I move."

Derrick shrugged his shoulders, not wanting to get Stackz started. He knew since childhood how his neighbor could go when heated, so he tried to diffuse any misunderstanding between the two by taking a cop off rip. "Come on, now; chill out with all that, fam. That back down memory lane history lesson ain't for me and you. We been better than that since. Now, I got you. And when I say I got you, then I *got* you."

"All right, then, dawg, don't let me down," he stated with a serious tone, deadlocking eyes. "We been rocking out a long time, Pissy, you feel me? And if you tell me you can make this go down, and you drop the ball . . . Put it like this; shit gon' get real ugly in the worst way possible, real quick. And just because you my cousin baby daddy, it still won't be personal, you know that, right?"

Pissy was shook, yet played it off as if he wasn't, taking the keys from Stackz. "Bro, I got this. Damn, I'm surprised it still turns over." Derrick turned the key in the ignition. ". . . as many holes in this baby. Shit, how did you not take one of these slugs?"

"I'm blessed by them hustle gods all day and damn night," Stackz replied while he drew an invisible cross over his upper body with his finger. "And, oh yeah, I need one more thing from you." Stackz paused and looked around the building at the various cars. "I need a whip. And not no tagged, stolen, or hot shit. I'm trying to make it home not jail!"

Pissy felt exasperated but didn't dare show it. Rubbing his head with his filthy hands, he looking around the building himself wondering which car was which and which ones actually were still drivable. Stackz expressed the fact he only needed to borrow the whip for a few hours, and he'd have one of his people meet up with one of his to return the ride.

"Okay, I got you, fam; say no more. Follow me." Pissy went through the door first. When Stackz stepped out the door, his supposed-to-be-childhood friend was standing next to a late-model Ford Probe.

"What the fuck is this?" Stackz barked, pissed off.

"This all I'm working with right now, baby. It's gonna get you where you need to, and it's low-key. Ain't nobody gon' suspect you to be in this right here," Derrick replied, trying to sell Stackz on taking the old struggle buggy. "I would let you borrow my personal, but, well, you know the paperwork on mine ain't right either."

Stackz shook his head in disbelief that a boss like himself had to be subjected to such a piece of shit on four wheels. Reluctantly opening the car door, he could tell by the worn leather on the seats the car's interior would smell just as it did—like stale corn chips and rotten cheese. Pulling off, he was exhausted and still hungry. He wanted nothing more than to go home and call it a night. Holding his breath as much as possible, hitting the freeway, he did just that.

CHAPTER SIX

Stackz made it home, thank God, without incident. Pulling the ready-to-be scrapped Probe in his two-car garage, he felt guilty leaving it parked next to his Range Rover. Finally inside, locking the door behind him, Stackz felt like he'd been through hell to make it back . . . and, in reality, that was not far from the truth. Immediately wanting nothing more than to relax and do what had to come on his list, he stripped all his clothing off before even leaving the living room. Going into the kitchen, he retrieved a huge trash bag from the cabinet. Heading back to the living room, he angrily gathered up everything he'd just taken off, including his shoes. Stuffing all of it in the trash bag, Stackz shook his head that one of his favorite shirts had to go. Sure, he had plenty of money to replace it, but he'd had it tailor-made right before the old Jewish man that owned the shop died. But being the thinker he was, he knew the outfit had to be got rid of. He knew the deal and knew CSI wasn't no joke.

After tying the trash bag up, he set it by the rear door so he wouldn't forget it when leaving again. Feeling like his body was still sweaty from the impromptu shootout in the parking lot, Stack knew it was about time for him to get right. Whereas some street players could go days without caring about their personal hygiene when they were on the grind trapping, Stackz couldn't cope. Money in the streets, business on the floor, or just going to run to the mall, Stackz prided himself on maintaining his

look; the persona that he was famous for. People might
have talked shit about him being a murderer, and for that
label being placed on him, he could care less. That was
true. Stackz had sent more than one motherfucker on his
way. But he'd made up his mind when he was a small kid
getting teased about the Salvation Army clothes he wore,
that when he grew up and got right, then he'd be all the
way right.

Going into the bathroom, he turned on the shower.
Just as Stackz got the temperature good and hot the way
he liked it, his phone he'd left on the coffee table began
to ring as well as his doorbell. "Fuck! Who the hell!"
Stackz said out loud to himself while snatching a towel
off the rack. Wrapping it around his lower body, he was
annoyed, hoping it wasn't the damn police. And if it
was, Stackz had decided not too long ago as he sat in his
prison cell that when he got released, there was no going
back. Come what may, he'd die in a hail of gunfire before
the man caged him back up like a wild animal on display.

Opening the cabinet beneath the sink, he reached
inside, retrieving one of many guns that he had hidden
around in his crib. Making sure it was loaded and ready
to clap if need be, Stackz returned into the living room.
There, he found his phone still ringing and the buzzer still
chiming. Snatching it up off the coffee table, he looked at
it and frowned. Realizing it's his brother and partner in
crime, Gee, he pressed the green talk icon on his phone.
"Get off my doorbell, nigga! Is you fucking crazy?" he
said, at the same time making his way to open the door.
"We don't do that ghetto bullshit out here in these parts!
What the fuck, fool, making all that noise? My neighbors
is respectable white folks with jobs and shit!"

Stackz was pissed that Gee was acting like an ass
ringing the bell like that, but knew what his reason
possibly was. Stackz could bet nine outta ten times, T.

L. had put him up on game and unlocked his brother's rage. He knew how Gee would get when pissed off. Just like him, he'd be hyped up; ready for war. That craze gene was embedded in their DNA. Before Stackz could get the door open good, Gee rushed inside on a hundred, almost knocking him down.

"Man, fuck all that! Miss me with your white neighbors! Bro, why the hell you didn't call me?" Gee said, pacing the living-room carpet, punching his left palm with his fist repeatedly, clearly agitated with his big brother's secret squirrel behavior. "Who was them lames that tried it? Was it Dae Dae and them or that faggot Clint?"

"Chill out, dude. I'm good," Stackz insisted, trying to calm his baby brother down. "It wasn't either of them cats. I'm a grown-ass man, and if I couldn't handle my own in these Detroit streets, I'd sit my ass down somewhere. Shit, get a job flipping burgers or something."

"Look, Stackz, all I'm saying is we got soldiers to get at fools. Dedicated-to-the-team li'l niggas ready to put in that work. You on paper. You can't go back to the joint now, not when shit popping off like it is. Thangs fucking good with business. I need you out here to help me think, keep shit together, you know what I'm saying, bro." Gee had his say before flopping on the plush leather sofa, finally beginning to calm down.

"Trust me, I know what you saying. I ain't trying to see the inside of nobody's cell again either, if I can help it. We out here in these streets, doe, bro, and shit is bound to happen; so if, and when it do, I'm gonna handle shit accordingly. If that means body bagging a duck, so be it. I ain't got no ho card a nigga can pull at will. Fuck I look like? I got this."

Gee stood up and got on damage control. "Dawg, you already know fam hit me and put me up on game. He did what he was supposed to do."

"Yeah, you right," Stackz agreed, knowing that's how their young soldier was trained to move.

"Yup, yup. He on his way out here now. Matter of fact, I'm about to call him and see where he at with the video so we can do this homework. We need to get on top of this shit like now."

Stackz still had the towel wrapped around his waist and still felt mad sticky. Seeing a mist of steam float out of the bathroom snapped him back to what he had to do. "Cool. Well, let him in when he get here. I'm about to jump in this shower real quick; then I need to take my ass to sleep. I'm spent, bro. But first things first, I wanna see my movie. I be telling ho-ass lames I'll make 'em famous," he joked as he walked away.

"Fam, where the hell you at? I'm already out here with this lunatic posted."

T. L. laughed, knowing Gee's assessment of Stackz was 100 percent correct at times. He could be a nut when need be. "Yo, chill. I'm about to pull up now. Shit, you might as well say I'm at the door, so come let a nigga in."

"What up, doe?" Gee barked, swinging the door open.

"You know what it is, my nigga," T. L. replied proudly, pulling the flash drive out of the inside pocket of his jacket, waving it back and forth. "See, you play checkers out in them streets. And a beast like me . . . Shiddd, I play chest," he taunted Gee. Always trying to outdo him at any and everything, whether it's serious business or just fucking around; the two knew it was all in fun.

"Fuck outta here, *li'l* nigga," Gee snapped with a smile on his face. "Remember who bestowed that swag on you son-son. I'm the original beat maker!"

"That's your story?" T. L. looked at Gee with a puzzled expression plastered on his face.

"Yup, and I'm sticking to it, lame," Gee replied while snatching the flash drive out of his boy's hand. "Well, let's get ready to peep this shit out."

"Where dude at?" T. L. questioned Gee before hearing one of the doors in the rear of the crib open.

Just then, Stackz entered the living room fully dressed, fresh out of the much-needed shower. Although he was exhausted, he was ready for whatever would have to be done after watching the footage. He greeted T. L., and then grabbed the television remote off the coffee table. Gee had already put the flash in the drive and was ready. He sat in the matching leather recliner chair and pulled the lever to raise his feet up as if he was about to watch a Netflix movie. Stackz then pressed play on the remote control and anxiously waited. The tension grew in the air as they waited for the television to go through the motions to start playing the main feature.

T. L. sat on a stool he'd grabbed from the kitchen. Rubbing his hands together like he was trying to warm them up, he anticipated seeing Stackz's reaction to be violent footage. The high-grade quality video began to play. It was clear Rank, Mickey, and Devin had been intimidating customers and raising hell from the time they walked into the restaurant. After watching the team of idiots clown and the back heads of two females that were sitting at the table with them, Stackz had enough. Picking up the remote, he fast-forwarded the surveillance up to the moment he walked in the restaurant in search of some chili fries. As Stackz watched, he felt enraged all over again, tasting blood boil in his mouth. In a matter of minutes, it was obvious the band of would-be thieves set their sights on Stackz.

Gee was momentarily silent, wanting to leap through the 55-inch flat screen and fire on one of the dudes that he knew was about to try his big brother.

T. L. showed his age as he loudly rooted Stackz on, as if he has looking at an action movie and wanted the underdog to win. T. L. yelled this and that at the television, waiting to see the part when ole boy he'd seen laid out in the parking lot got his ass handed to him.

Gee couldn't seem to contain himself or his emotions, either. Unlike T. L., who was just shouting obscenities at the otherwise silent footage, Gee leaped out of his seat to get closer to the big screen. Not sure this was real, he rubbed his eyes again and again. He couldn't believe who he thought he was seeing.

"Yo, back up, boy; we can't see! Back your big ass up. You not made of glass, motherfucker." T. L. moved from side to side, trying to make sure he didn't miss a beat of the feature film.

Gee gritted his teeth, shaking his head in disbelief. "Not these hoes," he blurted out loud with contempt in his tone. Standing with his arms folded across his chest, glaring at the screen, he was visibly heated.

Up until this point, Stackz had been quiet, in no way trying to celebrate having to put in felony numbered work. But easily recognizing his brother's demeanor, Stackz knew something was off. Hearing his last remark made him speak up. "What's up with you? You know these clowns or something, Gee? Put me up on game!"

Gee took the remote out of his brother's hand, then pushed pause so he could get a still shot view of the females. "Naw, the niggas don't register. But the females, yeah, I know them hoes. They sisters. That's Leela and Ava from our old hood we used to stay in."

"What?" Stackz frowned his face up as if to say, "Nigga, I don't know these broads."

"Naw, you was in the joint when they lived up the block from us. I've been fucking the bitch Leela off and on since I was in middle school. She the light skinned one with little ass T-shirt on."

T. L. busted out laughing at Gee. "Damn, dawg, she look kinda busted on this shit. Please tell me it's the lighting or the camera ain't catching her good side."

"Come on, nigga, ease up on all that. She just a neighborhood rat, and you know like most rats, she got a snapper on her."

"Whatever. From what I can see from where I'm sitting, she's just a waste of light skin. Give me the sister. Now, I'd break her back."

"Dawg, ole girl can be grimy. I done used her to get under a few niggas that had to be dealt with in the past. For a few dollars and some tokens for her kids to jack off at Chuck E. Cheese, she good to go." Gee ran down Leela's colorful, petty, and sometimes treacherous résumé, then followed it up with the 411 on her sibling as Stackz and T. L. listened carefully.

"Now, Ava, she ain't out there like her sister. Matter of fact, I'm surprised to even see her hanging with her sister and these bums. That bullshit is straight outta character. She usually be in her own lane. Last I know, she was deep off into school and running scripts out of this doctor's office she work at to finance the shit."

"Shit, you know like I do, any good girl got it in her to turn bad with the right dude whispering in her ear." T. L. acted as if he knew everything there was to know about every female that ever walked the face of the earth. Eager to please, he was thirsty for blood. "Look, just get me an address. I'll pay these bitches a visit and make sure they ain't gon' be a problem. I'll do my thang; I'm in and out just like that. I might even let schoolgirl suck my dick," he vowed with a sinister grin on his face.

"Chill, dude. They ain't no real threat. All I got to do is pull up on they ass and tell them what it is and they gon' follow the script. No problem," Gee pledged, trying to convince them his word was law with the sisters.

T. L. wasn't trying to hear what his homeboy was saying. He respected most of the moves he'd made over the years and always backed his play; but this time was different. He felt he had to push the envelope and go the extra mile. "Come on, Stackz, just give me the green light and it's go time on them broads. Gee dealing in his feelings, and this shit serious. These hoes can fuck up everything we got on the table just by placing a call."

Gee and T. L. argued with each other until Stackz had heard enough. He finally stood up, taking charge like a boss, barking orders to his right-hand and left-hand man. "Okay, dig this here. This what's gon' happen."

Gee sat back down, giving his brother his full attention. T. L. did the same, focused on his mentor, waiting for his instructions which would, of course, be law.

"Gee, I want to talk to these girls face-to-face. I'll be able to read the bitches then. Now, if I sense any fuck shit in 'em, then, T. L., you'll step in and do your thang. For now, let's finish watching this footage and see if we can place them fuck boys! After that, T. L., get on the horn, make sure everybody got that bread on deck, and if they need work, get 'em together."

After watching the action-packed footage several times and applauding Stackz's gangster themed-styled handiwork against three shooters, they came to the conclusion that none of them could put names with the faces of the idiots. Gee knew later on, one of the sisters, who were obviously riding shotgun, could do that—or risk T. L.'s impending wrath. Each having a mission to tend to, they all started moving around the front room. Gee paced back and forth, going through his phone until he found

Leela's number. T. L. got on his phone calling everybody holding a bag. Stackz found a pair of J's and stepped into them. After gathering a few things he'd need out in the streets—money, phone, gun, house keys, and, of course, an extra clip—he was ready. "Yeah, Gee, we in your truck today. I had to make my shit disappear," Stackz informed his brother.

"You better had, nigga, because that Commander famous all up in the video. Shit, them punks had your baby rocking back and forth, straight crying," Gee laughed, knowing his brother loved his Jeep.

"Fuck you, lame. Bet a stack niggas somewhere in the fetal position wishing they didn't go to that spot to eat doe or try me." Stackz reveled in coming out on top of the shootout. "And what did them females say? Did you catch up with them?"

"Yeah, we on deck, I told her I want a shot head, some bacon and eggs for breakfast, and I'm on my way. No argument. She with it as usual. A nigga say money, she all in. Plus, she ain't got no idea about you and didn't even mention she was out of the house last night."

Stackz popped the clip out of his gun, looked it over, then slapped it back in the butt of the gun. "That's what's up, Gee; let's ride!"

CHAPTER SEVEN

The two brothers sat outside in front of Ava and Leela's house. Gee took long pulls of some of Detroit's finest dispensary kush, getting his mind right. His voice cracked as he tried to talk while he held the thick smoke in his lungs. "I'ma go in first and see who all up in here; then I'ma come get you. It should be just them two, but knowing this rah-rah bitch Leela, you never can tell. I just want to make sure." As Gee exhaled the smoke, Stackz waved his hand back and forth, fanning skunky aroma.

"All right now, don't get in there and get all in your feelings over some pussy like T. L. said. We ain't got all day. We got money to get, so speed this shit up," Stackz said, looking out each truck window and in the rearview mirror. As he sat low in the passenger seat, Gee reached under the driver's seat with the blunt hanging out of the side of his mouth. After grabbing his gun, he stuffed his 9 mm in the waistband of his jeans under his shirt. Stackz watched his little brother walk up on the porch and knock on the door. Little did Leela or Ava know, but if things didn't play out right with Gee's conversation, it wasn't him, but death knocking on their door.

Leela was in the kitchen. She'd just finished scraping scrambled eggs out of the frying pan and onto a plate. Hot bacon and fresh toast sat on the table, ready to be served. Having a brief flashback seeing Devin laid out on the restaurant floor begging for his life, she heard a knock at the front door. Figuring it was her longtime fuck buddy

(F.B.) and every now and then come up, Gee, she fixed herself up best as she could. Trying not to look like she had been up all night crying, confused, and distraught, she wiped her face with her robe sleeve. Leela hadn't gotten a moment's rest because Devin's people wouldn't stop blowing up her phone, calling from Devin's, asking her questions and blaming her for his death. She just kept telling them to ask Rank and Mickey as she was fucked up in the head, in denial Devin was gone.

Still in hustle mode, with bills to pay, Leela made her way to the front door to let her potential meal ticket in. She took one last look at herself in the mirror hanging on the wall by the front door. Teasing her badly-in-need-of-a-touchup weave and loosening her housecoat, hoping she would be appealing enough for longtime F.B. to spend some cash, she schemed. Wearing no bra or panties, she was ready to serve head, pussy, and ass, along with breakfast, just the way Gee liked it; hot and ready. Of course, looking forward to a few dollars, which was sure to be tipped to her for her services and hospitality like always, it was game time.

Turning the locks and pulling the door open, there Gee stood, cocky as ever. "Bitch, what took you so long? My damn food betta not be cold," he lied, knowing full well food was the last thing on his mind.

"It's not, *boy,* and don't talk to me like that," Leela snapped with a playful attitude. Hugging him tight he gave her a dry-ass hug in return. She automatically sensed something amiss in his body language for a man about to get food and pussy.

"What's the matter, boo?" Leela quizzed, hoping not to mess up her soon-to-be-made and much-needed money.

"I'm good, ma. I just got some nothing-ass street bullshit on my mind. You know how it is," Gee said with a smirk on his face as he looked around the house for any signs of anyone else being there before he called his brother in. Seeing the scene was comfortable with no foul play in the air, he relaxed, adjusting his gun in his waistband.

"What's up with Ava? Where she at?" Gee wanted to know so an understanding could become between the both of them at the same time, wanting no misconception of how this situation was going to unfold . . . for their own good.

"She's up in her room, asleep, I think." Holding the door open, Leela could easily see Gee had somebody waiting for him out in his truck. "Who is that in your ride? You didn't say shit about no extra dick on deck. Now, I *know* you really gonna bless a bitch. Damn! I mean, I'll skull him up to, but you could have at least given a bitch heads-up. Do I know him?" Leela talked shit sounding like a true, uncut hood rat.

"Damn, ho, stand down," Gee commanded looking at her sideways. "That's my brother out there, and, naw, you don't know him—yet!" Thinking to himself he smirked, *But you going to.*

Leela got excited. She knew Gee was the shit, and if this was his brother, then she knew he was fly getting that paper as well. "Okay, then, cool. That's what's up! Tell him to come in."

"I will, but damn, girl, why you look like you've been taking dick all night? Bags under your eyes, and they all puffy and shit. What's up with that?" Gee knew what time it was. He'd seen her and Ava running out of the restaurant on the footage and just wanted to see if she was going to lie.

Leela sat on the arm of the sofa wondering if she should tell her fuck buddy what popped off the night before. Weighing her options, she decided to tell him only if need be. Gee knew she was banging other dudes, so she knew he would never be on that jealousy trip with her. But that trying to rob the next nigga . . . Gee would never ever condone that foolishness. Leela knew he lived and governed himself by a true gangster's code; get your fucking own and you'll always live long.

Gee's phone was going crazy ringing off the hook. He took it out of his pocket as he stood over Leela turning the volume down. "As a matter of fact, where that ho-ass buster you be running with? What his name you was fucking with the last time I came through and put it in your head? You know, the one blowing your phone up like a straight pussy!" Gee fished around, knowing it could be one of several dudes she ran with, hoping to push Leela into talking.

Off rip, she knew exactly who he meant. Distraught and not able to hide it, she held her head down, shaking it as she spoke. "He got killed last night fucking with the wrong nigga. It was so crazy how everything went down. It been on *Breaking News* all morning long!"

Gee knew this was about to be the moment of truth. These next few statements Leela was about to make would determine whether she and Ava would live beyond this morning. "Oh snap, for real? Damn, what wrong nigga was he fucking with? And shit, why he fuck with dude in the first place? You know that boy ain't never really been about that life."

On the verge of tears, Leela fought them off as she confessed her sins, so to speak. "Well, I was gone when it happened; after me and Ava got the fuck on. Dude was going to work on his ass. Thank God he let us leave."

"Say, word." Gee kept on playing the role, having had seen the entire incident inside the restaurant as well as the shooting in the parking lot take place earlier back at Stackz's crib, but he wanted to still hear her version.

"Yeah, he told me and my sister to get the fuck on. And you know me. I'm a survivor. He didn't have to say it twice, either. We was outta that bitch. Me and Ava ran as fast as we could to my momma house."

Gee would be lying to himself if he said he wasn't enjoying seeing Leela tell her tale. "Y'all ran to your mom's crib? Word?"

"Yeah, because she was like three blocks away from the restaurant we was at. You know, the one off Davison and Linwood. Shit, we wasn't trying to be a part of that dumb shit."

Gee stood in front of her with his arms folded, listening to her long drawn-out story while checking his watch for the time. "Yeah, I know the spot."

"Well, him and his boys was fucking with this dude that came in all fresh and shit. I mean, the guy looked like he was handling some real business out here, ya know. And, Devin, I really don't give a fuck about that nigga; he was just something to do. You know how I get down. Well, bottom line, he dropped the ball and the tables turned on his dumb ass. Now his sister and ole girl keep calling my phone questioning me like they the damn FBI. I told them I don't know shit. I wasn't there; ask his boys that was with him."

"Have the police got at you yet on anything that happened last night?" Gee continued to fish for more information.

"No, and if they do come at me, I ain't got shit to say. Fuck the police. I don't know shit. I ain't seen shit. I hate those bitches." She promptly reassured Gee that she wasn't nowhere near a rat, knowing snitches come up missing and found dead in the "D."

Gee had played the game with her and from what he could tell, she'd passed the test. He wanted to holler at Ava as well, but he hoped for both of their sakes, she'd follow her sister's belief values as far as the law was concerned. "Okay, well, dig this here. I'm 'bout to introduce you to my brother. And on that note, you better act like you got some damn sense. You feel me? Don't act a fool."

Leela was puzzled as to why he was acting like his brother was the president or some top-notch shit like that. "Why would I?" She turned up her nose watching Gee step out onto the front porch.

Outside, Stackz sat in the truck looking down at his watch wishing his brother would speed shit up. Just then, Gee appeared at the front door waving at him to come inside the house. "'Bout damn time," Stackz mumbled to himself. Wasting no more time, he hurried up and got out of the truck. Trotting up the stairs, he went inside as Gee led the way.

Leela stood up quickly when she saw Stackz come through her front door. She couldn't believe her eyes. She was scared. She was confused. She had no idea what was going on, and worse than that, what was about to go on. "Oh my God! Oh my God! What the hell is *he* doing here? Gee, that's the dude from last night! The one who did what I told you," Leela shrieked while carefully choosing her words.

"So we meet again, huh? That's right. I am the nigga from last night," Stackz snarled while moving toward her. "The one you and your crew tried to roll on!"

"Leela, shut the fuck up and meet my big brother, the one and only Stackz," Gee announced like he was royalty, grinning from ear to ear.

"Your brother? *He's* your brother?" Leela rambled on with her hand over her chest. As her heart pounded, it seemed as if it was going to explode at any moment. "How is this your brother? What the fuck is going on, Gee? I'm confused. How?" She didn't know if she should be scared or relieved that Stackz was Gee's brother as she closed her robe, which had fallen wide open.

Before Gee had the opportunity to respond, they each heard voices coming from outside in the front yard. Stackz, Gee, and Leela all stopped talking. Instinctively, Gee and Stackz reached for their pistols. Tension grew in the living room as the voices got closer to the front porch. At Gee's urging, Leela went to the window and peeked out through the blinds.

"It's the damn police," she turned, whispering over her shoulder.

It was indeed the Detroit Police Homicide detectives, along with two uniformed police. One of the uniformed cops was writing down the plate number on Gee's F-150. Little did the nosey, obviously on a mission cops know in reality, they'd turned on the block no sooner than Stackz stepped inside Leela's house. If they'd been one minute quicker, they would've been face-to-face with a killer now at large: Stackz.

"They coming on the porch," Leela stated wide-eyed, looking like she just hit a bump of crack.

"I'm out," Stackz said with conviction, sprinting toward where he thought the back door should be. With his hand on the knob, seconds away from opening the door, an officer appeared in the backyard looking at the door and windows for anyone that might attempt to leave the house. "Fuck" Stackz said to himself as he crept back to the front room avoiding any windows. "The cops in the backyard too," he announced to Gee and Leela in a low voice, looking back and forth at them both as to say, "What in the fuck should we do now?"

"Hurry up and go upstairs to my sister's place, just in case. There's a door in the basement that connects our flats to each other. We never lock the door 'cause we always up and down all the time," Leela explained to the man responsible for killing Devin and injuring both Rank and Mickey. But like she'd told Gee, fuck the police. She wasn't a rat and didn't assist rats, either. Let them earn them blood money paychecks.

"Go, bro, we got this." Gee motioned with his hand like a nigga would do when they trying to make his boy move fast to avoid getting caught by the police.

Following Leela's directions how to get upstairs, Stackz made it to Ava's after going down one flight, then up another. He entered through her kitchen slowly as not wanting to startle her. The on parole murderer had no intentions on Ava clowning like Leela had when she saw him and possibly draw the police upstairs. He'd first have to assure her he meant her no harm. How he would accomplish that, Stackz didn't know. In his head, as he navigated himself through her crib as quietly as possible, he'd cross that bridge when he got to it. On a side note, he noticed she had a clean, well-kept house; the total opposite of her sister's spot, which looked and smelled like a low-rate cathouse. How his brother Gee banged that bottom-feeder Leela was beyond his grasp.

Stackz couldn't ignore this place smelled so fresh and clean. She had good taste in furniture, nice pictures on the walls, a flat-screen television in her front room, and clean carpet throughout the house. Stackz was impressed, to say the least, not expecting Ava to have it going on like she did. Still moving with caution, he heard music playing low down the hallway that he soon discovered led to two bedrooms and a bathroom. Getting closer toward the rear of the house, he heard running water coming out of the bathroom and a strong mist of steam. Suddenly, the sound of running water stopped.

Stackz stopped as well. Standing dead still against the hallway wall next to the bathroom and the partially opened door, Stackz peeked inside. He saw Ava rubbing a towel over her caramel, wet, well put together body.

Normally a boss where the females were concerned, Stackz had to catch his breath. Quickly ducking back up against the wall, shocked and aroused, Stackz's dick got hard seeing flashes of Ava in his mind from the restaurant, fast-forwarding up until now. He thought he was kinda attracted to her the night before, but he knew now for certain.

Ava was lost in her own world as well, listening to the music that way playing on the radio. Opening the bathroom door, she was unaware of Stackz's presence in the hallway. For all Ava believed, she was alone in her home; carefree with no worries. However, that was about to change.

Out of nowhere, a strong force grabbed her around her waist, yanking her backward. A hand covered her mouth and before she knew it, she was lifted off her feet. Terrified to death, she attempted to scream and resist, yet it did her no good. She was overpowered by her mystery attacker. As Ava's eyes bucked, a voice with a warm breath whispered into her ear, "Calm down. I'm not going to hurt you."

CHAPTER EIGHT

"Who in the hell beating on my fucking shit like they dun lost their goddamn mind?" Leela roared, yelling through the closed door.

"The Detroit Police Department," one officer loudly replied from the front porch, gun in hand.

Gee sat calmly down on the tattered sofa, but not before brushing a few random crumbs off of it. Holding a small wad of cash in his hands, he nodded his head. "Welp, you up, bitch. Earn your fee," he sideline coached Leela like she was next in a pickup basketball game at a city court. Leela rolled her eyes at him. When she said she hated the police, she meant it. That statement wasn't for show; it was a fact. After the cops had the nerve to bang once more like they paid her bills, Leela snatched the door open, then proceeded to go ham.

"Okay, I know I just really woke up and might be tripping, like I'm hearing thangs. But which one of you disrespectful fools beating on my door like you live here? I mean, why? For what?"

One officer in a hand-me-down Goodwill suit decided to cut straight to the chase. "Yes, miss, are you Leela Westbrook?"

"Yeah and . . ."

"Well, Miss Westbrook, we're investigating a homicide that took place early this morning."

"And what would some damn homicide have to do with me?" Before the policeman could get another word out, Leela leaned over toward the right side of the gate, locking it, showing her contempt for their unwarranted visit. "Look, Officer, I don't know where you got your information, but trust me when I tell you I don't know jack shit about no murder this morning or any other time."

The detective was not giving up so easy having gone up with other supposed witnesses to crimes that claimed to have seen nothing. "Hold on. You haven't even heard the victim's name or know the location so—"

Still not trying to hear what Joe Law was saying, Leela went back in. "Look, I done told you I don't know shit about no damn homicide. Period." She purposely allowed her robe to open. "Now, if you talking about how to suck a good dick or how to throw this hot pussy on my man, then lock my pretty ass up. I'm your girl. 'Cause see, I'm all the way on my job. Otherwise, y'all might need to go look elsewhere."

Seeing they were getting nowhere with the defiant female, the detective left his card, asking Leela to please give him a call within the next twelve hours or he'd be back, and next time, they wouldn't be knocking.

"Whatever. Scat." She dismissed the policeman and his colleagues off her sister's property. After closing the door, Leela marched over to Gee with her hand stuck out, expecting not only the money in his hand, but some dick as a tip. Sure, she was sick about Devin being dead and his murderer upstairs with her little sister, but she still had to get her money by any means necessary.

Stackz held Ava firmly in his arms. Wanting nothing more than to break free, she struggled as if her life depended on it. And for all she knew, it did. The soft powder-blue towel wrapped around her trembling body fell to the floor. Naked as the day she was born, Ava still tried relentlessly to get away. Being ashamed of her nude body never crossed her mind until she saw her reflection in the full-length mirror at the end of hall that hung on the outside of the bedroom door. Not only did she see herself, she saw her attacker as well—the guy that gave her sister's hanging buddies the business. The man who Ava had heard ended up killing Devin after they fled the restaurant and wounding Mickey and Rank.

Shocked, she stopped resisting. If Stackz wanted to have his way with her, then so be it. She wanted to live, and if it took giving up the cat, she'd not put up a fight. Coming to her senses about who he was, what she saw him do, and she was naked, she had no win. The thought in her mind skipped to, *Is this fine-ass nigga gonna kill me after he get the pussy, or what?*

Stackz felt Ava's body go totally limp. Not wanting to scare her any further, he reassured the naked beauty once more in a cool, even-toned voice that he wasn't going to do her any harm, and that she could relax. "Seriously, chill out, ma. This ain't what you think it is. I ain't trying to hurt you, I promise."

Ava found her second wind and tried to buck a few more times, while biting at Stackz's hand which was still wrapped around her mouth. "Let me go, let me go," she managed to muffle the words from her covered mouth.

Stackz's big strong hands pressed against her lips were only tickled by her bites. The more Ava squirmed, the more he secretly liked her determination to get loose. "Look, I swear I will let you go if you stop embarrassing yourself," he announced, hoping she'd calm down. Feeling Ava's hot, naked body up against him, Stackz fought with himself for his dick not to rock up. "Hey, Gee is my brother," he whispered in her ear as she squirmed once more in his arms. "You know Gee; he grew up with you and Leela."

The words Stackz spoke took Ava by surprise. She stopped moving as if she was trying to comprehend what he'd claimed. The fact a dude she and her sister have been cool with since childhood has a brother she has never met, who is the same guy that she thinks is fine as hell, but has her hostage and killed Devin a few hours ago, took a moment to penetrate her mind.

"Listen up. Your sister and Gee are downstairs talking to the police right now. That's why I'm up here. Leela said it was cool." Stackz hoped he had gotten through to her, and she would stop bugging out. "Okay, now, if I let you go, can you please act like you got good fucking sense? I ain't trying to have the damn police run up here. That ain't what I need, or what you want."

Ava nodded her head the best she could, mumbling yes. Stackz did as he said he would and prayed for both of their sakes she'd keep up her end of the bargain. Just like that, Ava was free from his strong-arm hold. Finally free, she didn't yell or scream. She didn't run toward the bedroom or bolt in the kitchen to grab a knife. Instead, a baffled Ava turned around and just stared at Stackz speechless.

After a few brief seconds realizing she was naked, Ava became modest and began to blush. "Oh my God!"

Stackz stepped back, looking Ava up and down. "I see God blessed you from head to toe." He shook his head slowly in utter amazement.

Ava took her time bending down with her mouth twisted and giving Stackz the side eye. She grabbed her towel off the floor and wrapped it around herself. Then she pranced across the hallway toward what had to be her bedroom. She stopped at the doorway only to say, "Let me put some clothes on, if that's okay with you. And then you can explain how you and Gee are brothers, and we never met you before now."

"Go ahead, girl. Put some clothes on that perfect body. A nigga will be right here waiting." Stackz grinned, wishing she'd invite him in and bang his lights out.

Secretly, Ava was intrigued with Stackz. He had a swag that meant business; he stood upright, and dressed like he had his clothes custom-made. In between last night and now, Ava could tell whatever he was into, this guy was straight winning. Slipping on some sweatpants and a T-shirt, she then quickly stepped into her sneakers. Brushing her hair back, Ava felt ready to face Stackz and anything else that was to come her way today.

When she stepped out of the bedroom into the hallway she expected to see Stackz standing there, posted, waiting for her. However, she was fooled. He was not there. Praying that he'd not disappear as suddenly as he'd interrupted her morning, Ava walked to her living room. There, she found Stackz lurking near her front window. Assuming he was watching the cops pulling away from the house, Ava asked him what was going on outside just to verify. Stackz insisted to her that everything was good and that they should go downstairs so they could all four get some things straight. Although he felt a good chemistry between them, Stackz was still not opposed to sending Ava or her sister Leela on their way if they wanted to go against the grain about the forced-hand restaurant shooting.

The pair took the same way down to her sister's as Stackz had taken coming up. Neither said a word, but both could tell this was possibly the beginning for the two of them. That is, if Stackz was who he said he was, and he believed that she wasn't anything like her sister and her foolish comrades. They found Leela and Gee in the living room mocking the police and shooting the shit about how dumb cops are these days to think anybody would help them do their job. Leela had just repeated something slick she'd said to the big-bellied officer before dismissing them from around the perimeter.

Gee looked up, seeing his brother and Ava coming through the kitchen and into the dining room. He smiled when he saw Ava was unharmed because he knew Stackz didn't give a damn about shortening her or anyone's existence on earth if they couldn't be reasoned with. He was a man with zero tolerance for bullshit.

"All right, now, Ava, I see you've met my brother for the second time and in less than twenty-four hours," Gee casually remarked.

The sisters attacked, bombarding them with question after question. "Why we never knew about you?" Ava suspiciously asked with folded arms.

"Yeah, Gee, you never talked about or mentioned no other brothers, other than that crazy ass, T. L. Now, out of the thin blue sky, another brother pops up," Leela chimed in with her two cents.

Ava was blunt and direct, saying, "Look, if he's your homeboy, that's cool. We, like, been knowing you forever; we get it. You fell through with yo' man to let us know he with your crew. Enough said, we ain't cut with rat in our DNA." Ava looked at Stackz and Gee with a serious expression on her face that said, "Don't play with me; I'm not that bitch." "So if that's the reason for this visit, y'all good my way. I mean, it's fucked up Devin's dead. I feel for his family. But I never liked his grimy ass from jump. That's Leela's people, not mine."

"Damn, Ava, just throw me under the fucking bus!"

"Naw, it's not like that, sis. I'm just saying he was an asshole that liked to dominate and hit women. And a nigga like that is bound to get fucked up with dealing with a real alpha man. RIP, Devin, but damn . . ."

Gee, like Leela, took notice Ava and Stackz were looking at each other with a hint of lust. They didn't know what was said upstairs when they first met, but whatever it was, the two were giving off strange vibes now. Leela read Ava like a book and knew that her sister was feeling Stackz. That man that'd killed Devin after pointing a gun at them as well. The same man that tried to take Mickey out of the game and almost blew Rank's wig back.

When it had come to relationships, Ava had always gotten men that did for her without her asking and treated her with the upmost respect, but never a man with any real bosslike qualities Stackz seemed to have. Leela had always harbored jealousy toward Ava for that; not to mention her younger sister was prettier and a low-key hustler, getting her coins without having to sell her ass. She always paid her bills on time and didn't wait on no man to do for her. Ava understood the power of her pussy and possessed a strong mind to back it up. A man could never sell her a dream. Unlike Leela, Ava wasn't in the market to buy off into bullshit

As the four of them came to an understanding that Stackz was not looking for any trouble the night before and had no choice but to send Devin on his way, Leela's phone rang. Looking down at the screen, she saw it was Devin's sister yet again calling from his cell phone, surely to harass her about her dead brother. Leela was tired of going back and forth with her. She'd already informed her and his mother she was not there and had left early. Leela had already begged them to ask Mickey and Rank if they didn't believe her, but I guess that would be too much like right. Fed up, and, of course, wanting to show out in front of Gee, Leela answered and was ready for verbal combat.

"Damn, bitch, what the fuck you want? Why you keep calling me? I already done told your dumb ass!"

Devin's sister had a better idea other than going back and forth on the phone; she wanted blood firsthand, or so she thought. "Dumb ass? You got me fucked up. Bring that ass outside, you dirty, set-up, nut-guzzling ho!" Devin's sister yelled on the phone. "Everybody knows how you get down setting real niggas like my brother up to get got! You ain't slick, bitch! Not at all!"

Leela was heated. She sprinted to the front window and looked outside. Sure enough, Devin's entire 285-pound sister was pacing her gorilla ass back and forth in front of her 2007 two-door, rusted-frame Neon.

"Come on out here. You talked all that rah-rah on the phone, you slimeball-ass bitch. You set my brother up, and you know it. You gotta come out sooner or later. I'm posted out in this bitch." Devin's sister had no chill or off button. She was going at the top of her lungs, not caring who heard or saw her. "Mickey and Rank scary asses acting like they don't know shit, but I told the police to come over here. Your good dick-slurping ass was probably the one who pulled the trigger!" All she knew was her brother was dead, and the last time she'd seen him alive, he had Leela's conniving ass hanging on his arm.

"Oh hell to the naw. She want it, she can get it." Leela darted past Gee, going into her nasty bedroom. Grabbing a pair of leggings and a T-shirt out of a huge pile of dirty clothes thrown off into the corner, she quickly put them on. Putting on her high-top sneakers, Leela was hyped. She didn't tolerate no bitch coming to her front door talking that beast-mode shit—dead brother or not. Running back into the living room it was definitely on!

As Leela was passing back by Gee on her way out the front door, he snatched her up by the arm. "Yo, girl, hold up. She just in her feelings about her brother, that's all. The bitch just venting!"

"Well, let that rotten-mouth-in-her-feelings trick call Dr. Phil's baldheaded ass or go vent somewhere else. This motherfucker over here is a straight no-vent zone!"

Stackz had just about enough of hearing Leela talking trash, that good shit about how she was that real deal. Even though he hoped no one called the police before he left, he wanted to see if her turn-up was official. "Naw, bro, your girl wanna be all that; let the shit ride!" After coaxing his brother to let her go, Stackz grinned, waiting for a potential battle royal to jump off.

"Yeah, Gee, let me go. I don't give two hot shits if your brother sent her brother on his way last night. She still ain't gon' come over here going for bad, like I pulled the trigger. Fuck her and fuck him too! She wanna act like she about that life—well, so the fuck do I." Leela pushed the gate open, boldly marching out onto the front porch. As if on cue, Leela began snapping on the biggest female she'd ever had to face. Even though she was unsure of the outcome, that still wasn't gonna stop her from going hard, especially in front of an audience. Win, lose, or draw, Leela felt confident because she had two of Detroit's most gutter niggas in her living room, along with her sister cheering her on.

Threats were thrown back and forth amongst the lightweight and heavyweight thots. Suddenly, it was as if each of them heard a bell ring. Leela sprang off the porch, and big girl moved into action as fast as her tree trunk legs would allow. They squared up like pro MMA fighters. Big girl swung first, missing Leela's head because she ducked. Leela caught ole girl with two quick punches to the side of her head, but fat girl was unfazed. She closed her eyes, swung wildly, rocking Leela halfway to sleep. Leela couldn't recover from the blows to her face and head. She fell down, and Devin's sister had her right

where she wanted her—underneath, with all her weight
pressed on top of her. All Leela could do was shield the
attack.

Ava had seen enough. Sister or not, she secretly didn't
mind seeing Leela get her ass beat; she just didn't deserve
this ass whooping. So, of course, Ava did what any real
sister would do . . . assist Leela. Unlike Leela, she wasn't
about to play no games at all with Big Bertha. Ava politely
walked off the porch. Reaching over, she swooped up one
of her sister's kid's tricycle by the handlebars. Walking
fast with deliberate intent, Ava saw red as she cocked back
the tricycle with one hand, aiming it at the female's head.
Bringing it crashing down, Ava hit on target. Instantly,
blood squirted out of the top of big girl's head. With her
skull cracked and leaking, it slowed down her assault on
Leela, but didn't stop it altogether. Ava then picked up a
piece of wood that was thrown on the side of the vacant
house next to theirs. Gripping up, she swung the thick
board like an ax, hitting the side of her neck. This time,
big girl was fucked up. Allowing Leela to breathe, she fell
over on the ground, wounded, exhausted, and wanting
no more trouble. Blood was in her eyes and covered her
face as she got up, stumbling to her car. Before she pulled
off, she promised both Leela and Ava that she'd see their
asses again.

Ava scraped Leela up off the ground, helping her
in the house. They went straight into the bathroom
where the light was good. She inspected her sister for
any serious wounds. Despite all the blows she took,
Leela managed to only have a few scrapes and bruises
and a swollen eye. Her pride was more hurt than anything else. Talking shit while she got herself together,
Gee was dogging her out about having got her ass
handed to her, and that Ava was the real MVP of the
family, having to save her big sister's ass.

Ava sat down on the sofa crossing her legs. With folded arms, she was still heated from the drama that'd just taken place. She hated beefing with females, and now, because Leela wanted to go for bad, Ava too now had beef looming in the street. Stackz sat close to her as she tried calming down. He wanted to sit around and kick it with her, and if they were maybe upstairs in a cleaner environment, he would've. However, he was pressed for time, knowing he had business on the floor. Stackz asked Ava if she had a phone, and she smartly replied, "Don't everybody?" He laughed, and she laughed as they exchanged numbers. The pair agreed to hook up sooner than later, and with that exchange, he hollered for Gee to bring his ass; the streets were calling.

CHAPTER NINE

T. L. was out and about in the streets of Detroit from east to west, picking up money. Everywhere he went, people were talking about the shooting at Legends Coney Island on the West Side that left one dead and two others shot. After T. L. kept hearing people talk about the shooting, he wanted to know what the police were saying, but didn't have time to go look at the news because he had bread to get out of the mud. So he did what any street nigga on the move would do: pulled up "Crime In The D" on the gram for the latest updates on crime in the city.

The police chief always made his presence known on the page making comments to the media about what actions were being taken and preventive measures against crime. Sure enough, at the top of the page, T. L. got the info he wanted; which was, there were no suspects. No video of the incident because of equipment malfunction and the victims, along with restaurant employees, have no concrete description of shooter or getaway vehicle.

After calling Tangy, telling her he wanted to give her some of his dick for a job well done, T. L. called his man, Stackz. "Yeah, dawg, the streets is definitely talking about what jumped off. That shit even on the gram, but from what I saw, that nigga Devin was a setup dude; straight slimeball, ya' feel me? If it wouldn't been by your hand, then it was coming soon anyhow."

"I ain't never gonna cry over having to send a lame on they way for stepping to me wrong, but fuck. A nigga like me was trying to live right; stay out here for a few. See how y'all live in the free world!"

T. L. quickly informed Stackz he had his back, and all he has to do is give him the green light on anybody, and they were as good as dead. "Look, fam, you don't even have to worry about all that. I got you on this, I promise. Them other two fags ain't about shit to a player like me. I'll be in and out. Make the shit simple." He begged Stackz to let him go to Receiving Hospital to finish Rank and Mickey off. He swore to Stackz adamantly that he wouldn't disappoint him or let him down. "I know you been gone for a long time, family, and you know it's all love and nothing but respect, but I'm grown now. I'll put in that work for you, no doubt. I ain't just about that life; I *am* the life."

Stackz saluted his gangster. He told T. L. he was proud of him and glad to have him on the team; that he was the son he never had but wished he did. "Man, I'm telling you I love your loyalty. You always got ya manz best interest at heart, and that shit is rare as fuck. But if you make a high-profile gangster move like that, shit would only bring more heat and slow up how we getting this paper, which is unacceptable." Stackz then gave T. L. more directions to follow as to who to go take big packages to and where. They ended the phone conversation by saying, "One," showing a sign of unity amongst them.

Stackz got off the phone with T. L. "Yo, that young boy is a straight savage. We raised a damn animal out there. But one thing for sure, two things for certain . . . He a team player like a motherfucker. He ready to go burn down the police station, if need be, and stand outside with the matches when they run out."

"Dawg, T. L. wild, that's for sure," Gee agreed while lighting up a blunt.

"Well, one good thing; he told me the streets is talking. We knew that much was gonna happen. But they ain't got no clue who did what. Them ho-ass niggas must be keeping they mouth shut and not telling the police shit."

"Yeah, true that. And T. L. got Tangy under control. Ain't no loose ends. You good!"

Giving Gee the serious side eye from the passenger seat of the truck, Stackz rubbed his hands together as if he was scheming. "Maybe, maybe not. I mean, on some serious shit, how much you really know about Ava and Leela? I'm saying, can they be trusted, or is all that 'we down, we down' bullshit just a front? 'Cause like I said, I don't mind killing a bitch; even one as fine as Ava."

Gee was quick to give his big brother the rundown so he could ease his mind. "Okay, now, Leela, she ain't as smart as Ava. You can already tell that much before she even opens that good dick-sucking mouth of hers. Leela problem is she fucks with dudes to get what she can out of them far as a few dollars and be way too loyal to the wrong motherfuckers. She been like that for years."

"My point exactly, so if she can be bought so easy, who to say she won't sell me out to Crime Stoppers or the next nigga in the city with that cheese?"

Gee replied with a smile on his face. "Come on, now, what crew in this city got more paper than us?"

"True that." Stackz gave him some dap.

"Look, bro, if she show any signs of selling out, she dead; her and Ava. I don't give a fuck how long I been knowing them hoes. You know how we do!"

"Dig that." Stackz sat back, hoping what Gee claimed was indeed credible.

Gee hit the blunt twice more before tossing the tail out the window and continued his rundown of the sisters.

"Now, Ava, like I said, got her head on hustling. She going to school to be a pharmacist or some shit like that. She works at some doctor's office part-time over around the way. Girl be getting the doctor's scripts and flipping the shit outta them bad boys. Ava can get it all; anything . . . OxyContin, Vicodins, Norco, and Xanax. You name it, bro. Oh yeah, and she owns the two-family flat they living in. She bought it all on her own at an auction."

"Well, that explains why her crib looks like heaven, and her sister's crib look like hell. But, damn, nigga, if you all like Ava for president and shit, why you hitting Leela's nothing ass off instead of baby sis?" Stackz was just trying to keep it real with his little brother, wanting to know the true reason. "Is she gay or something? I mean, why? Put me up on game!"

Gee couldn't do anything but shake his head. He often thought about how he got caught up with hitting Leela off too, instead of Ava, but the reality was simple. Leela had been giving out free pussy and head passes to guys in the hood since she was eleven, maybe twelve. Ava, on the other hand, was a schoolgirl focused on nothing but her studies. And after her older sister had blessed a guy, so to speak, Ava didn't want any part of their tainted selves. Gee included.

"Naw, dude, she ain't gay, not at all. She just one of them females that don't entertain that bullshit. She a good girl, always have been, ya feel me? And besides, you know I likes them freaks!"

Stackz had seen the type of females his brother would bring around and knew what he was saying was true. Much like T. L., they always went for the crazy-as-hell, window-busting, shit-talking, razor-blade-in-their-weave, let-me-have-some-money-for-this-pussy-type of women. That was their thang. "Yeah, well, what's up on them pills? She got you plugged or what?"

Gee sped up, nearing their exit off the freeway, "Naw, bro, here's the thing. Ava been said she'd hook me up, but when I fall through and try holler at her, Leela always manages to find a way to put my dick in her damn mouth. I ain't bullshitting, dawg, and by the time she done sucking me dry, a guy too tired to discuss business."

"What the fuck!" Stackz laughed at what Gee was telling him. "Are you serious, fool? Too tired to talk about making money? Nigga, miss me with all that. You betta boss up. Let me find out you out here shittin' on the family name!"

"Nigga, I'm telling you, Leela skull game dangerous; she got skills; crazy swallow-a-nigga-whole skills." Gee turned looking over at Stackz. "And yeah, I peeped the way you was rocking with Ava. You just betta hope that shit ain't in they bloodline, 'cause the same shit might happen to ya ass too!"

Stackz immediately gave Gee the *imagine that bullshit* expression. "Dawg, I ain't cut like that. Ain't no pussy or head better than getting this money, you best recognize. And as for Ava, if she act right, I might just touch the bottom."

"Okay, now, fam, I'm telling you, it's some serious skulldullery going on over at that crib." Gee mocked his brother one last time as they pulled up at their destination. "Okay, Stackz, you've been warned."

It had been nothing short of sheer pandemonium for the three best friends since deciding to try Stackz. If they would have just kept minding their own business, ate their food, and left like everyone else, things may have been different. If Rank and Mickey could turn back the hands of time, one of them could have been man enough to stand up to Devin and convince him that all money wasn't good money. That each had looked at Stackz, sizing him up, and could easily see he was not like the other customers that'd come into the restaurant to grab a late-night, early-morning meal. Devin should have seen that much for himself, but either was blind to the fact or just didn't give a damn. Whichever of the two factors that made him jump for bad had caused him his own life and almost the lives of his two follow-the-leader henchmen.

Dressed in soft powder-blue scrubs, the technician working the day shift aided Rank back to his room. With her assistance, she helped him up into his hospital bed in the Emergency Room. Thanks to Stackz attempting to peal his cap back, Rank had a deep, inch-long open wound from the bullet, narrowly penetrating all the way full force. Having just come back from x-rays, the doctors advised Rank that had he'd been hit a mere three centimeters over toward the right, he'd be downstairs in the refrigerated morgue, laid out alongside his friend.

Rank's head wound was thoroughly cleaned before they put three staples across it and a white gauze bandage. Having one of his eyes semiswollen shut and his front tooth missing from diving face-first onto the ground to avoid any more of Stackz's return fire barrage of bullets, Rank was sore all over. He had the worst headache of his life, almost wishing he was dead. Lying back in hopes of getting some rest, Rank replayed the entire avoidable incident in his mind. He knew Devin was wrong as two left feet and knew he and Mickey were misguided for running out in the parking lot trying to be hard, but it was what it was and is what it is. Stackz had killed they manz and one day, someway, Rank vowed revenge to the nigga that'd almost took his life as well.

Out loud through a cracking voice Rank mumbled, "RIP, bro; he gonna pay. Can somebody please get me a charger for my phone?"

Upset and snapping on people because they only had iPhone chargers and he had an Android phone, one of the young nurse's aides went to the gift shop and bought him a charger. Finally, he powered his phone on, and fifteen text messages from Leela popped up, back to back to back. As Rank read through texts, Mickey walked into his room with his arm in a sling and his shoulder patched up. Since the bullet went in and out, he was able to sign himself out of the hospital and be on his way. They greeted each other and shared a deep sense of shame knowing they got fucked over and their boy body bagged; all three by one man.

"What are you on? Who are you calling?" Mickey asked Rank, who was focused on looking at his cell.

"Dude, Leela has been blowing up my phone and texting the shit outta me. Devin sister came up here on the nut before I went to take x-rays. You know she going ham about, bro."

"Word," he replied while trying to adjust his sling a little bit more comfortably.

"You know she was going through it down here. His entire family was. Did they come in your room?" Rank looked up waiting for an answer as he still talked. "She was all up in my damn face like I killed his ass. And as soon as I even mentioned Leela's name, she went ape shit with her big ass. Dumb bitch wouldn't even give me a chance to tell her Leela didn't have jack shit to do with it, but she wasn't try to hear nothing else I was trying to say. Last I know, she was headed over to Leela's house on some rah-rah shit. I was trying to call and warn Leela; give her a heads-up."

Mickey could only shake his head, not being able to imagine what Devin's family, especially his mother, was going through, waking up to the news no parent or loved one wanted to receive. "Naw, I didn't see them, but the fucking police came to my room. But you know me, I played the amnesia role on they ass and said it was some random nigga we never seen before just started spraying the parking lot. I sent them packing, but they ho ass said they was gonna get back at me later! Man, fuck 'em!"

"That's right, nigga," Rank agreed, snarling his face at the business card Mickey showed him. "Fuck the damn police. We gonna handle this shit street style; for Devin. Now, let me call this girl real quick before ole girl pull up over there on some ambush shit and get to molly whopping bitches."

Unfortunately, by the time Rank was able to get through to Leela, it was too late. Blaming the delay on poor reception in the hospital, he apologized, knowing how Devin's sister had gone ham on him as well.

"Yeah, the tramp was over here trying to go on me, but you know that type of shit don't fly in this jurisdiction. Flat out, her big, triple-cheeseburger-eating-ass thought she wanted it, but ended up getting it," Leela bragged while placing a cold rag on her eye, hoping the swelling would go down. "When you see her, ask her how that head doing. You know that fool left here leaking! Shit, she probably on her way straight to the hospital, ole dumb bitch! I told her I ain't have shit to do with Devin getting killed but—"

"I already know." Rank cut Leela off before running down his firsthand account of what transpired after she and Ava were given a hood pass to leave the restaurant.

After hearing everything Rank said, she was heated at Devin for being so stupid to go outside like he was Scarface and Stackz for doing what he was truly supposed to do; protect himself and life at all cost. Leela couldn't help but think that the man who took Devin's life had just been in her house. *This the same nigga that sat on my sofa, took a piss in my toilet, and I lied to the police about—Gee's damn brother! What the fuck!* Leela wanted to tell Rank and Mickey she'd found out who Devin's killer was quicker than both of them and the police but decided to wait. Not because she gave a fuck about any of the parties involved. It was all about her and how the information could benefit her.

Rank's headache was intensifying. Telling Leela they would meet up and talk in a few days once things settled down, she agreed, and they ended their conversation.

CHAPTER TEN

Ava went from her bedroom to the bathroom getting ready to go to work. She'd been up all evening studying and thinking about Stackz. Every time she walked down the hallway, she imagined him snatching her up in his arms. She thought she could feel the strength of his body weight against hers, pressing her on the wall as she tried to break away. Taking a deep breath, Ava inhaled the intoxicating scent of Stackz's cologne that was still very much lingering near her bathroom door. Normally, she'd spray air fresheners or burn scented candles; but not last night and not this morning. Strange as it seemed, it was as if the man she knew was a murderer of at least one man, and God only knows how many countless others, had her mind spinning. They'd exchanged numbers, and as bad as she wanted to call, she knew it would be in her best interest to just kick back and play the role. If it was meant to be with Stackz, then it would be; one way or another.

Taking a break in between daydreaming about a man she didn't know, Ava thought about the plays she would make later when at work. That was, if the risk factor was low. Knowing she had to keep an eye on that old nosey bitch, Ms. Heath, who was always in her business, Ava stated devising clever and innovative plans to get her away from her desk and into another part of the building so she could do her dirt. Ava had figured out the first week on the job working at the doctor's office, that Ms.

Heath was the one person in the building having keys to every single door, locked shelf, file cabinet, and medical supply dispensary in the entire place.

Finally heading out the door, she jumped in her car and backed out of the driveway. After getting a call from her mother saying that she needed some extra money for groceries to feed the kids, Ava grew infuriated. She was tired of receiving these desperate-sounding 911 calls from her mom about needing money for this or that where Leela's kids were concerned. It was bad enough that her older sister had multiple baby daddies that never ever step up to buy a diaper, a bike, a birthday gift, or even offer a ride to the doctor's office; that was between Leela and her children. She'd have to face them later on down the line in life and explain her poor choices of choosing a man that was a deadbeat father. But Leela was, of course, receiving food benefits for all three of her kids, plus herself. And selfishly, instead of doing the right thing, which would be hand the card over to her mother who kept the kids most of the time anyway, Leela would sell a small portion of it. After doing that, she'd spend the rest on feeding herself luxury food items and various snacks that her many men would eat when falling through to check her out.

As Ava drove, she grew angrier thinking about all the chaos and turmoil Leela had delivered to her front doorsteps since she allowed her to move in downstairs. If it wasn't one thing, it was another. If her sister hadn't been evicted from the place she and the kids were staying at in the dead of winter, Ava would have most certainly let her go to the shelter like she'd done so many other times since purchasing her home. But no, her mother had connived Ava so she had some sort of mercy for her sister and sympathy for the kids. She'd given in, having been promised by Leela she'd be quiet as a church mouse and be gone in ninety days. Well, it had been an entire year last week on Tuesday, and Leela was still camped out in the lower level of the dwelling, loud as could be, filthy as ever, and cocky as ever, showing no signs that she was even considering leaving. She'd basically dumped the kids over at her mother's house after the first month of living at Ava's. She claimed she was out looking for employment, when, in true reality, the only thing she was looking for daily on the regular was some dick.

Unlike her sibling, Ava wasn't about that life and never claimed to be. She just wanted to go to school, go to work, and come home to a tranquil environment. But just like the prior evening, Ava let her guard down and hung out with Leela and her band of idiots. And what happened to her peaceful existence? It was abruptly ruined. She'd had a gun pointed at her, police knocking at her front door, a strange man snatch her up naked in her own house, and a Class-A beef with a dead man's big-boned sister. Shaking her head, she tried to get her suddenly messy life out of her mind as she called her mother back to tell her she'd get with her after work.

Ava's hustle would not be stopped. She'd gotten five scripts so far today and flipped that well worth over a thousand bucks, all going straight to her pocket. Stuffing her ill-gotten gain into her purse, she smiled, thinking about buying some new living-room furniture later on in the week. As she stood in the bathroom mirror mapping shit out, she couldn't seem to get the last twenty-four hours out of her mind or the new mystery man that came along with the crazy night.

Not wanting to step on any toes or have any more unwanted beef with females in the street, Ava decided to do her homework. Still not sure if she should have any dealings with Stackz if and when he called, she knew what to do to answer that question. She called her girl that knew everybody's business you could imagine. She stayed keeping her ear pressed to the ground. Word was, if you want to know anything about anybody, ask Bridget.

Ava placed the call, and she and Bridget talked about the normal shit; who was fucking whose man, who was broke, who had a new car, and what color weave the neighborhood ho had in her head this week. Ava knew more than likely her own sister Leela was the topic of Bridget's gossip fest on more than several occasions, but who was Ava to judge? She knew the way Leela ran around town passing out pussy and running with jerks, she was gonna be the star of Hot Topics at least twice a week, if not more.

Having had her ear talked off more than twenty minutes or so, Ava couldn't take it any longer. She had to know what was up with Stackz. Cutting Bridget off in midsentence about Devin's sister and Leela fighting, Ava bluntly asked her the million-dollar question. "Oh yeah, I almost forgot, do you know a fine-ass dude name Stackz? I think he be getting that bread, or at least he look like he do."

Her girl was turned up instantly, responding with what Ava wanted to hear: the 411. "Girlllll, yessssss! What bitch out here on the hunt don't know or ain't heard of Stackz? Shidddd, he like heaven out here in these streets . . . *long* paper." Bridget was too geeked as she broke his hood résumé down to Ava. "And, girl, I hear his fuck game got hoes going crazy. I mean, like *crazy crazy,* you feel me? Oh my God, why you asking me about that king? You got the dick, girl? Please tell me you got the dick! You lucky ho! Is it as big as bitches be saying it is? Tell me." Bridget was going a mile a minute, throwing question after question in Ava's direction, hoping to get some dirt and gossip to take back to the next person she spoke to.

Putting Bridget out of her misery, Ava simply answered no, deflating her wagging tongue. "He came by the clinic today, claiming that someone sent him to talk to me saying I had the hookup on some pills." She lied about their meeting. After all, it wasn't like she could tell big-mouthed Bridget the truth. "I just told him I didn't know what the hell he was talking about and sent that boy on his way. He was fine and all, but I don't know him and damn straight wasn't gonna do business with no stranger. Shit, for all I know, he could've been the damn police!"

"Ava, that's ole boy I was telling you about awhile ago. I tried to get you to remember, fool!"

"Girl, with work, school, and hustling hard, I don't pay these men much attention. You know me." Ava tried to play it off, not wanting to drop her hand.

Bridget was still excited hearing Stackz's name and was not ready to let the conversation go that easy. "Girl, he's Gee's brother; a few years older than him. I used to talk to the younger brother T. L. a few years ago, but he didn't turn out to be shit."

Ava had heard enough gossip from Bridget as far as Stackz was concerned. However, she allowed her messy informant to go on and on about who the rumored "big dick kingpin" used to kick it with when he came home from jail and what he did to get locked up in the first place. Ava was certain if it wasn't time for her to get back to work, Bridget would have told her Stackz's Social Security number and what color boxers he had on today.

Leela had been feeling under the weather for the past few days, but this morning, she'd become violently sick. She jumped out of bed and ran to the bathroom, barely making it as vomit sprayed the floor and toilet seat.

After throwing up much of her stomach's contents, she was weak, not having the strength to stand to her feet. Distraught and in tears, she crawled back to her bed with the taste of vomit lingering in her mouth. Climbing up in the bed, the mother of three pulled the covers over her head. She'd been down this road before, knowing deep inside, she was pregnant . . . again.

After resting awhile, she got up and went to purchase a pregnancy test from Walgreens. While she was in line to pay for it, along with a bottle of juice, Devin's sister that she'd fought came inside the store but, thankfully, headed directly to the pharmacy to pick up a prescription. Leela wasn't scared to come face-to-face with her once more, but she knew the last thing she needed to be doing was bucking in her weak condition. She wanted to confront her and reiterate that she had nothing to do with her brother's death. Yet, after reminiscing about the last time she tried to do that, she changed her mind. Putting her bag into her purse, Leela cowardly slipped out of the store not wanting to be seen.

When she made it home, Leela went straight to the bathroom which still reeked. She opened the box and removed the white indicator stick. No stranger to these tests, she set it on the sink, then pulled her leggings down. Leela looked on the floor because she'd stepped in something wet. Getting queasy again, she realized being trifling, she hadn't cleaned up the vomit from earlier. Yanking a dirty towel off the side of the tub, Leela dropped it on the floor, stepped on it, then used her foot to mop the chucky foul-smelling mess up. After kicking the vomit-drenched towel off to the side, Leela sat down on the toilet and peed on the stick.

Leela was mentally fucked up; she sat on the toilet with both hands over her face. She didn't want any more kids and knew she didn't have time for the ones she had. She had her life to live, and she was good with seeing her kids over at her mother's house occasionally.

She snatched the test off the sink and stared at it. *Damn!* Sure enough, the test read positive for her being pregnant. She cursed God out for what she believed he had done to her. In her mind, she never did anything wrong to deserve all she'd been through lately. It wasn't fair. Life wasn't fair. She couldn't believe it. It couldn't be true, but this was the same test she'd used over the years, and it had never been wrong; ever. *I'm fucking pregnant!* The symptoms she was experiencing were dead giveaways.

Leela's first thought was to get an abortion like she had so many other times in the past. But she was 99.9 percent sure this baby was Devin's, which meant it was the only thing she had left of him. In that very moment, Leela planned to fuck over Stackz and anyone else riding with him. That included Gee.

CHAPTER ELEVEN

Thankful and looking forward to getting some rest, Stackz had finally made it back home. Looking in his garage, he happily took notice that Pissy's ridiculously out-of-character loan he was forced to borrow was gone and back on the grounds of the chop shop where it should be next in line behind his beloved Jeep to get melted down into nothingness but a block of untraceable scrap.

Stackz was glad he had a team around him that knew how to follow orders and did what needed to be done in a timely fashion. In his line of work, time was of the essence. It had to be if he hoped to stay two steps ahead of his thirsty competition. Putting his key into his front door, he stepped through the threshold ready to take off where he'd left off when last home; go directly to bed. Stackz wanted to take a hot-ass shower and relax. So he did just that. Naked in all his glory, he laid his seven-to-twelve-years penitentiary-cut frame across his pillow top mattress king-size bed. He closed his eyes and replayed the last twenty-four hours in his mind.

Never pressed over any female he'd come in contact with, he couldn't seem to shake the vision of Ava naked and in his arms. He thought how good he felt holding her, not only in a forceful manner, but how good it would feel if Ava didn't resist.

Sure, he could fuck any ho that was always on his jock, but that was the problem; they were hoes. Stackz was good at reading women because he has run through so many. He could tell Ava wasn't like them, and for that, she was worth checking out. Stackz wasn't wrong much when it came to figuring what a woman's true motives were and was never a sucker for pussy. As he lay there thinking about Ava, seconds away from drifting off to sleep, Stackz continued to keep in mind, less than twenty-four hours ago, she and her sister were running with a nigga that he forced to take a permanent nap in the dirt.

CHAPTER TWELVE

Leela was on her way home from taking her benefit card over to her mother's house and visiting with the kids. Her mom had been calling her and calling her like she was crazy, claiming they had no food in the house to eat. She knew her mother was running game half the time, just trying to get Leela over there so she could have a break. Deep down inside, Leela knew she was dead wrong and she needed to spend more time with her own children, but her life was too hectic for the young mother of three to slow down and care. Like Ava, she wanted to go out and have a good time and have a good man spoil her; go to school; have a job; be well respected; own her own home. But that wasn't in the cards for her. Leela hated the nothing-ass life she'd created for herself and hated her sister even more for not following in her footsteps. Misery loved company, and Leela was standing all alone.

"Yes, excuse me, but are you Miss Westbrook?" a flower deliveryman asked as Leela approached her front porch.

"Yes, I am, how can I help you?" she asked with excitement, knowing what he had in his hands was obviously for her.

After asking her to sign for the long white red-ribbon-tied box, Leela stood at the top of the stairs elated. She finally had someone to care about her. She didn't know which one of the many men she banged on the regular had blessed her, but it didn't matter. These flowers were just what she needed to yank her up out of the funk she'd been in since Devin's death, or murder, as she often referred to it, as when speaking to her sister. Easing the small envelope off the ribbon, Leela opened it and read the card out loud.

Ava, Steak or Lobster? Diamonds or Pearls? Your choice. Call you soon. S.

Leela was heated. Jealously kicked in. Her blood boiled. She thought back to how their mother used to make her wait on her little sister hand and foot. That right there was the original root of all the hate and resentful feelings toward them both. Leela had a love-hate relationship with most of the people in her life, and there were no exceptions.

Fuck you, nigga. Leela wished Stackz could hear her thoughts after reading his note to Ava. "And for you, bitch, ain't gonna be no damn joy in your forecast today, little Ms. Sunshine. That's a wrap!" Lifting the lid on the trash can, Leela maliciously tossed the whole box of flowers inside before closing it down. Storming up the stairs and onto the porch, she slammed the door shut, not once looking back.

Ava was at the doctor's office and couldn't get her mind right. She found herself fucking up on her hustle, knowing that was costing her money. She not only sold scripts, she also put together doctor excuses for a fee. Preoccupied, she'd messed up two different women's paperwork and had to spend double the time correcting them. Knowing she had to be on top of her game when it came to dealing with the official doctor's excuses as well as the scripts for this pill or that, Ava fought with herself to get it together. The more she tried, she just couldn't get Stackz out of her head. She reflected back to him holding her tight close to his body and got chills.

She closed her eyes and was back in the hallway naked and afraid, yet aroused by Stackz polished thug demeanor. She wanted to believe she was tripping when he had her pressed against him, but thought she felt his dick getting hard. And if she did, it felt thick and long. Like he had said, God blessed her. If what she felt between his legs was real-life true, God had blessed him as well. Knowing she had to get back in the zone, she got Stackz out of her mind, then stole another few scripts.

Ava came home from a long day at school and work. Pulling up in front of the house, she got instantly annoyed. It was bad enough her sister didn't pay any bills around there and had no problem playing her music loudly into the wee hours of the morning. Most days, Ava didn't trip on that. But the thing that always got her heated was Leela would have nothing-ass people hanging out at the house that seemed not to give a damn about where they'd toss their garbage. They would leave trash in the yard and all on the porch like they thought they were at a park in the hood. "I swear I'm gonna throw this chick out one day. All I ask this girl to do is take care of the house, and she can't even do that."

Ava set her work bag on steps and began picking up trash in the yard. With a handful of paper, along with a beer can, she opened the trash can lid. Seconds before tossing the debris inside, Ava was taken aback about what she was seeing. She wondered who would dump a box of fresh flowers in her garbage can, of all cans. Seeing the envelope thrown on the side of the box, lying on top of a half-eaten apple, Ava wanted to be nosey and reached inside to pull it out.

The ecstatic emotion Ava was feeling, that Stackz was thinking about her and had made the first move, was short-lived. She was livid, knowing there could only be one person that petty who would've taken flowers meant for her and thrown them away: Leela's bitter ass.

Her days are numbered around here! Ole rotten, can't-get-right bitch! Ready to do battle, Ava headed to Leela's door and let herself in. No sooner had she stepped inside the threshold, Ava cut off into her always-known-to-be-spiteful sister. "You come-drunk slimeball, why the fuck you throw my flowers in the trash that Stackz sent me?"

Leela put on a real show, acting like she didn't know what Ava was talking about. She claimed she'd never seen any flowers and blamed it on one of the neighbor's kids.

"Really? One of the neighbor's kids? You must think I'm dumb or something. You just jealous like you always been. Shit don't make no kind of sense. I'm so tired of your bullshit!"

Leela was in defense mode but still tried to cover her tracks. "You know what, Ava? Fuck you! Ain't nobody jealous of you or them dumb-ass ugly roses! And you tired of me? I been tired of you too!"

"Well, guess what? Since we both so tired, how about you get all your shit together and GTFO! Beat it! I'm done!"

"What, bitch?" Leela shouted back. "Really? That's how you gon' do me?"

Ava laughed as she headed out the door. "Yeah, Leela, I'm gonna do you just like that. And for the record, if you didn't know anything about any flowers, how did you know they were roses?"

As Leela stood there busted, looking stupid, Ava rolled her eyes and reinforced that she was done, and sister or not, Leela had to start to find another place to live. Leela set the back of Ava's head on fire with her eyes.

Ava sat in her bedroom thinking about her and Leela having words. She felt like she'd done all she could to help her. Thank God neither of them was dead from the constant drama Leela kept them in. Ava loved her sister but couldn't understand why she was always so envious of her. She recalled when they were teenagers, Leela was putting out, but Ava wasn't. And, of course, Leela gave Ava's boyfriend the pussy. That moment changed everything between them for life. From that day on, she never trusted her sister around any man that she was dealing with, knowing Leela had no boundaries.

CHAPTER THIRTEEN

T. L. sat in his rental car at the corner of Rank's block, watching his house like a hawk. Some of his boys had put him up on where Rank and Mickey were posted at most days. Wanting to be as thorough as he could when putting in work, he studied their every move. If they went to the corner store, McDonald's, or even the gas station for a swisher, he followed. When Mickey visited his grandfather in the nursing home, T. L. was there. When Rank thought he was sneaking around the block to get some late-night pussy from the next bitch, T. L. was there posted as well. T. L. smoked a blunt and listened to his music to get his mind right. He'd paid good money for these fools' address, and from the looks of things, he was getting his money's worth.

He'd been on post watching them come and go all day and half the night. Seeing them together, one with an arm sling, the other with a bandage on his head, T. L. laughed, flashing back to seeing them on the video bloodied, defeated, and running for their lives. It took everything in him not to flick the fully auto switch on the Mac 90 that was in his lap and shut the block down. And when they went into the house, T. L. fought not to just walk up to the front door and knock on it, and when they opened the door, force his way in and lay everybody in the house facedown. At this point, Rank and Mickey were living off pure luck because all Stackz had to do was give T. L. the green light, and they'd be toast.

T. L. called Stackz, telling him exactly where he was at. After talking for a brief moment or two, Stackz praised him for finding the location of the soon-to-be-dead cohorts of Devin. Suggesting to T. L. to not make a move, but instead, continue to keep a keen eye on them, T. L. was low-key disturbed he wouldn't be putting in any real work on them, but kept his true feelings to himself. He knew Stackz was the leader and trusted him to do just that—lead.

T. L. slid down slowly in the driver's seat as he talked on the phone to Stackz. He seethed with fury as he gave him play-by-play of what he was seeing. The police detectives had just showed up at Rank's house and appeared to be asking Rank and Mickey questions. As they stood outside in the front yard, T. L. watched each person's hand gestures and body movements. He couldn't hear what was being said, if it was good or bad. However, regardless, being seen even talking to the police or saying good morning to their crooked asses ain't ever been a good look in the law book of the streets.

Stackz and T. L. went back and forth over whether he thought Rank and Mickey were standing strong keeping their mouths shut like real niggas in the streets were supposed to do in the face of trouble, or were they being full-blown rat pussies doing the homicide detectives' job for them. Not knowing for sure what the conversation was, selling the idea to Stackz that they had to be bagged and toe tagged to ensure his continued freedom was not an automatic go. Stackz told T. L. to use his head not his gun all the time. He explained that if Mickey and Rank had any intentions of telling what they knew about Devin's necessary death and their being shot, the damage was already done. If not, just fall back. Their time to die would be coming soon enough.

T. L. agreed with Stackz as he cracked his car window a little bit more seeing some sort of commotion starting to pop off. Leaning over toward the window as much as possible, the detectives could be heard raising their voices at Rank and Mickey.

"Okay, it's fine with me if you two don't mind taking up space in the already overpacked city morgue. When you lying on that cold-ass steel table, you'll wish you would've talked then so we can get this monster off the streets," one detective smartly remarked as he turned walking away toward their car.

Not to be outdone, his partner chimed in, cosigning on what they knew Mickey and Rank's near future more than likely held. "Yeah, let's go, Bob. We'll be back to either arrest these clowns for murder or notify their people where they need to go to identify their bodies. Fuck these assholes and all that no-snitch bullshit they adhere to!"

T. L. watched the police skirt off, livid they'd have to actually do some real detective work themselves to earn their paychecks. It was clear at that point in time neither Rank nor Mickey was giving the cops information on who killed their boy. The cops pushed it to them that by doing so, they were causing enormous medical bills to rack up that neither would be able to pay; least not in this lifetime.

T. L. put his mentor up on the theatrics that had just taken place and what was said by the cops. Stackz praised T. L. once again for being a true soldier. He then advised him to keep tabs on Rank and Mickey as best he could, but first and foremost, take care of his own business getting that bread and keeping the ticket straight.

Inside of Rank's mother's house, he sat at the dining-room table all fucked up; his head bandaged, eye swollen, and stitches in his face. His pride chewed up, spit out, and stomped on. Mickey fared no better, his arm in a sling from a bullet hole in his shoulder the size of a half dollar, and every time he breathed in or out, he was in pain. On top of all that, every time he blinked his eyes, he could see Devin's face turn into blood and bones. Since hiding behind that Dumpster, Mickey had nightmares of being shot at by Stackz repeatedly. He wanted revenge, hoping some type of "get back" would stop the torment he was going through in his mind.

With a floral-designed hijab covering her head, Rank's Muslim mother sat at the table, Quran in hand. Trying to convince her son Raakin, or Rank, as he was known in the streets, and Mickey, to tell the police what they needed to know to catch the person who killed Devin, she prayed. She'd known Devin since he was a young child and knew he'd been trouble since back then. She never wanted her son to hang with Devin, but Rank was grown and had other ideas about how he was going to live his life. Asking them if somebody killed them, wouldn't they want somebody to be brave enough to speak up? With no filter, they each got disrespectful with their response.

"Damn, Ma, you need to stay out of our business. Fuck the police. They don't really give a damn about us. They glad Devin's dead 'cause he's one less nigga they gotta deal with out here. You think they really care if they find whoever did that? Hell naw! They don't, but I do, and ole boy that hit me gonna pay with his life!"

"Yeah, Mrs. Muhammad, you want us to be labeled rats out in these street and miss our chance to be real niggas? I don't think so. I'm not going out like that."

Rank and Mickey looked at each other in agreement. They made a pact that as soon as they were healed, they'd hunt Devin's killer down and make him pay with his own life.

Ashamed and horrified they would speak to her like that, Rank's mother shook her head and put her hands over her face. She knew all she could do was pray for them and put it in Allah's hands.

CHAPTER FOURTEEN

Two weeks had passed since the shooting took place, and all was going smooth for Stackz and Ava. They talked on the phone and texted each other just about every day. Business was always on the top of Stackz's list, and school and her job consumed most of Ava's time. They had finally agreed to hook up and go hang out over the weekend. It would be their first time alone together since Stackz had her held up naked in the hallway. Each of them looked forward to spending time with the other.

The weekend had finally arrived. Stackz had been going hard in the mud getting money so he was feeling himself. He'd gone shopping and bought new gear to throw on, and like always, from the crispy fitted Detroit baseball cap down to his fresh out-of-the-box Tims, Stackz was in full hood star mode. Ready to stunt, he even broke out his Versace iced-out chain and bracelet with the pinky ring to match.

He'd told Ava he would pick her up about nine o'clock. It was only eight thirty, so Stackz sat in his living room with the Detroit Pistons game playing on the big flat-screen TV on mute. He had a thousand-dollar bet with his boy that the Pistons would beat the Lakers by at least six points and was starting to second-guess his wager.

Placing a call to his boy, Maestro, the head bouncer at Detroit Live, Stackz chopped it up, letting him know he'd be falling through tonight and for him to hook up a VIP booth with black bottles on deck. Maestro assured him he'd have him together, like always, whenever Stackz stepped through the door.

Letting his brother know where he was gonna turn up at tonight, Gee agreed to meet him there and have T. L. and the young boys on deck, in case any madness popped off. Stackz looked at his watch, seeing it was time to roll out. He shut everything off except the front-room lamp and headed out to pick Ava up. Having got it detailed earlier, Stackz was driving his Range Rover just to hurt his haters' feelings tonight. Backing out of his driveway, he was feeling good and eager to chill with Ava. Since meeting her, she's played at his mental and his manhood. In other words, Stackz wanted to show Ava why he's talked about amongst more than a few bitches in Detroit.

Many women called Stackz a womanizer, even whorish, but yearned to be his bottom chick. However, to him, that coveted spot had to be earned, not sucked up or fucked up on. Stackz wanted a woman that could mentally connect with him. Of course, he hoped Ava was that one.

Stackz pulled up at Ava's house. Taught never to blow your horn for a woman, he wanted to get out and knock on the door, but knew somethings in some hoods weren't safe; especially if there were full-blown beefs jumping off. Opting to call her, he let Ava know he was outside. Being asked to give her at least five or six more minutes, Stackz placed a few more calls, checking on some traps he'd set the earlier part of the week.

Ava was almost ready. Nervous about her first actual date with Stackz, she darted from the living room to the bathroom to the bedroom doing what most women do when they were rushing. Knowing that Stackz was parked outside waiting, she picked up the pace trying to get out the door. Dressed in a short but respectable white form-fitting dress, she wanted to look her best for the man her chatterbox friend Bridget had boasted about. Agreeing to get a room with Stackz for the night was straight out of character for Ava, yet taking in consideration the way in which they met, nothing they did or said to each other would be unconventional for the couple.

Even though she and Leela weren't on the best of terms, her older sister volunteered to help Ava with her hair. Spending time assisting her to pick out the perfect pair of shoes to wear, loaning her a small clutch purse she'd shoplifted some time back, and even advising Ava on what bra and panty set she thought would drive any man nuts, Leela was going beyond the call of duty.

Something she never did if it didn't benefit her.

With Leela, there was always an ulterior motive involved in her day-to-day tumultuous life. For every action, whether big or small, Leela had a reaction; most times, an overreaction. This night was no different as her blood boiled. Secretly, she was livid having not been invited to join her sister clubbing. Of course, she hated Stackz, but loved being out in the streets having a good time more. Leela knew Gee would be there, along with their other crew members, spending money, flossing popping bottles, and turning up. It wasn't fair. She wanted to turn up too. Leela didn't care if she was knocked up. She'd partied when pregnant with all her other babies, and they turned out okay.

While Ava put her makeup on, Leela snuck downstairs calling Gee. Right off rip, she cut off into him, bitching about not taking her out with them. Gee couldn't believe she had the nerve to call him like that. He'd never risk tainting his boss status reputation actually being seen out in public with the city-known slut bucket. She was an in-house hit; nothing more, nothing less. After letting Leela have her say, Gee proceeded to dog her out, telling her she was his Tuesday late-night, dick-sucking bitch and today was Friday. Leela hung up the phone on him as he laughed with his homeboys that were in the background, cheering him on.

Returning upstairs under the pretense of continuing to help her baby sister get ready, Leela stood in the bathroom doorway making casual conversation, asking Ava where the turnup was for the night. Thinking nothing of it, she told Leela that Stackz had said Detroit Live on the riverfront, or something like that.

Leela walked Ava to the door, telling her to be careful out in these Detroit streets as she got in Stackz's truck. She had a wicked half-cracked smile on her face as she stood on the porch watching the truck's taillights drive out of sight. Taking her cell out of her back pocket, Leela was done playing with both Gee and Stackz. She was going to put her plan in full motion to see them both fall . . . hard.

Leela closed the door, then plopped down on the sofa. With sinister thoughts, she dialed Rank's phone number. When she got through to him, she asked him to hold on while she got Mickey on the line as well. After making the three-way connection, Leela started making some life-changing confessions that would affect all three of them. Without leaving anything out, she ran down everything that had happened with her since that night Devin got killed in the parking lot.

Revealing she knew the man that had murdered Devin and pushed it to both of them, Leela heard nothing but dead silence on the line as she spilled her guts. She ran down almost minute-by-minute the chain of events that followed the second she and Ava ran out the doors of the restaurant that awful night up until a few seconds ago when Stackz pulled off from the curb. Leela lastly announced that she was pregnant with Devin's baby and was going to keep it, so they'd both better get ready to stand up and look out for their boy's seed since he wasn't here to do it himself.

Leela claimed she wanted to say something sooner but was worried about her sister getting caught up because she's been dealing with Devin's killer. "Yeah, I'm not gonna front, I was confused as hell and scared. But, fuck that nigga. He killed my baby daddy, so, yup, fuck him! If y'all wanna holler at Stackz tonight, I'll tell you where he gonna be at and what type of ride he in; that is, if y'all trying to have a real gangsta moment in memory of Devin!"

"Good looking out, Leela. We going down there tonight and lay on that nigga. See what's really good with him." Rank had paced the floor throughout the entire call. "So, Mickey, get ready. I'll be there to get up in a few."

"Hey, y'all, don't hurt my sister when y'all do what y'all do. I told you she riding with that asshole." Leela pretended as if she truly cared one way or the other if Ava caught a few.

Rank and Mickey assured her that her sister would be good, even though they thought it was foul Ava was running with the dude that'd killed they homeboy and father of her sister's baby. Leela ended the call with them and went into the kitchen craving ice cream. Taking a big bucket of Butter Pecan ice cream out of the freezer, she went back to the couch. Opening the lid, Leela calmly stuck her spoon in deep and went to work like all hell was not about to break loose. *Oh well, it is what it is. Let the bullshit begin!*

CHAPTER FIFTEEN

Rank pulled up in front of the place Mickey had been staying at. After blowing the horn twice, Mickey ran outside, jumped in the car, anxious to put in work. They both were more than angry the fool that'd murdered Devin was fucking with Leela's sister, of all people. Rank as well as Mickey dragged Ava's name and character through the mud to the fullest. Although she never hung with their crew on the regular, they felt like she betrayed both them and Devin. Now, armed with this information, it would only make good sense to be extra careful what they said around Leela. She might've called, giving them the 411 tonight, but it had taken her so long to do so. For now, they'd use her to get closer to getting at Stackz if tonight didn't go as planned.

Having a heads-up on Stackz's location, Mickey and Rank jointly agreed there would be no gunplay tonight unless absolutely necessary. The game plan on tap would be to simply get a closer look at their enemy. Rank and Mickey were far from real true players in the Detroit underworld. After Leela gave them a name to work with, Rank got in touch with a few people that knew a man, who knew a man. After several calls, the trap house workers spoke to someone that ran the streets and could officially put them up on who Stackz was and what he was about.

The information they received was deeper than they could ever imagine, and they regretted that Devin's brief attempt at having a "gangster moment" with Stackz had brought the devil himself knocking at their front door. However, having to answer the door on point and principle, they got their courage up. Discovering that Stackz was no slouch and the type of respect he'd garnered in Detroit, Mickey and Rank knew whenever they were to make a move on Stackz, they couldn't slip, stumble, or fall—or they'd suffer the same fate as Devin. Not fully physically at a hundred from their last battle with Stackz, both felt it would be all good to go to Detroit Live, because, after all, they were just going to smoke the nigga over tonight; not kill him.

Rank's adrenalin was in overdrive, having flashbacks of Devin taking his final breath as he watched, helplessly perched behind a car leaking from the head. His hands were sweaty, and his heart raced as he gripped up on the steering wheel. Sure, he'd found out Stackz was somewhat a boss of bosses, but he had no other choice but to clap back. It was the law of the streets; at least, in Detroit. Besides, he couldn't look at himself in the mirror if he didn't.

No question, Mickey was shook but tried to play it off as he held the passenger seat down. He'd already been shot by Stackz once and definitely didn't want to risk getting hit again; even grazed. Caught deep in his emotions, Mickey knew he was lucky to be alive. Low key, after getting word from the streets exactly who Devin's killer was, he really wanted no part of Stackz anymore. However, he wasn't going to leave Rank hanging, who seemed so gung ho to get revenge. Taking a pint of gin out of his pocket he'd been sipping on earlier, Mickey twisted off the cap. Hoping to ease the pain in his shoulder, he took a long, hard drink and swallowed a few pills. He nervously gagged, and his eyes teared up. Wiping his mouth with the sleeve of his shirt, his liquid courage was in full effect. He then bravely grabbed his pistol out of his waistband, mumbling something about revenge as well. With his arm fresh out of the sling, the coward street soldier was ready for war.

In an attempt to hide the bloodstained bandage wrapped around his head, Rank threw on an Old English D knitted hat that was in the backseat of the car. Ready for whatever was gonna happen after whatever came next, the pair of would-be gangsters shared the rest of Mickey's gin. With murder on their minds and Tupac blasting through the speakers, they were on their way; destination: Detroit Live.

CHAPTER SIXTEEN

Stackz and Ava turned right off Jefferson Avenue. Making a quick left, then another right onto a side street, they were at the Detroit Live Nightclub. Immediately seeing the block was packed with cars bumper to bumper, Stackz started feeling himself. Instantly, he got a rush of excitement, knowing he'd be the talk of the club tonight, just as he always was. As he leaned over in the driver's seat, letting the crowd of potential partygoers jock not only him but the whip he was pushing, he fought back the urge to smile. Ava, on the other hand, was far from playing the cool role. Like a small kid in a candy store, her eyes bucked twice their normal size. Amazed so many cars were parked around the club and in the lots, she knew it was going to be at least a good hour or so before they could even think about getting inside, if at all.

"Damn, it's jumping around here! But, Stackz, look at the line to get in the club. You sure we should go here? We can go somewhere else. It really doesn't matter to me."

"Line? What line?" he teased, looking at the front door of the popular club.

"Come on, now. I know you see all these people out here waiting to get in. It's crazy. There must be about a hundred folk, if not a little bit more."

Stackz was amused at her innocence. It was apparent she either didn't know who he truly was or was good as hell at playing the role. Either way it went, he felt he had to set her straight. "Dig this here, baby girl. Bosses don't do lines. Me and mines VIP everywhere we roll."

"For real?" Ava replied not knowing what else to say to his gangster-inspired impromptu speech.

"Yeah, Ava, for real." Stackz reached over, grabbing her hand. "If you didn't know before, you're gonna find out tonight how I get down."

Stackz brought the triple-black Range Rover to a complete stop directly in front of the club entrance. Without hesitation, he pulled out his cell phone. Scrolling through his long list of contacts, he finally hit the talk button. As he watched his boy work the crowd of clubgoers, he couldn't help but laugh out loud at seeing some random nigga get tossed on his head.

"What's so funny?" Ava asked, staring out the passenger window at a flock of hating-ass females. "Do you know these thirst traps?"

"Huh?" his attention was brought back to her.

"These bitches over here acting like they lost something up in this truck." Ava was starting to show her true hood colors as her face frowned up, remembering what Bridget had claimed the rumor was around town about Stackz.

He glanced out the window to see what and who Ava was talking about and laughed, "Oh, them birds! Hell naw, I don't know them. And even if I did, they can't hold a candle to you. They're not even in your league. Matter of fact, can't no woman stand in you light; not tonight!"

Ava calmed down and eased back in the passenger seat. As far as she was concerned, no female had to like her. She knew the world didn't work like that. However, they'd definitely respect her. That much went without saying.

Stackz held the phone to his ear and watched his boy snatch another dude out of line with one hand, then sling him across the concrete. After he slid a few feet, security was on him, beating his ass. They dragged him up the street and left him there, coming back to their post. Stackz's boy Maestro, the head of security, barked at the crowed asking them if anyone else would like to join dude up the block. No one said a word, acting like they hadn't seen a thing.

Maestro finally pulled his cell out of his pocket answering it. He and Stackz talked shit back and forth about the dude that just got his ass stomped. He told Stackz to park his Range Rover right in front of the club in the no-parking zone, assuring him not a soul would look at his whip wrong without paying with their life. Stackz boss maneuvered into his parking spot as Ava looked on, impressed, to say the least.

Stackz turned off the truck and got out, straightening his clothes. People in line stared, whispered, and some wondered who he was that made him so special to get top billing parking. Stackz came around to the passenger-side door, opening it. Appreciative to be in her company, he took Ava's hand, helping her down out of the luxury model SUV.

As they walked hand in hand toward the entrance, Ava overheard a girl ask her friend if that wasn't that Stackz. She quickly replied it was and wondered who that bitch was that was with him.

"I swear, these thirst traps are out tonight with no shame at all. Your groupies might need to fall the fuck back, because I won't be disrespected by none of your thots," Ava warned with a sassy stern tone of voice.

Stackz would be lying to himself if he said he was not thoroughly amused by Ava's spunk. "Calm down, bae, they ain't nobody. Who I'm with?"

Gee and T. L. called out Stackz's name. They were with three guys and two females that were on the payroll.

Once the entire crew met up with Stackz and Ava, they were eager to get inside the club and get the night started. Stackz grabbed Ava back by the hand, leading the way inside.

Once inside of Detroit Live, not one of them was searched, not one of them paid. To Ava's dismay, the Middle Eastern owner of the club came to personally greet Stackz and his entourage with open arms, like they were family. Stackz had two VIP booths and plenty of black bottles were already set up for him and his people.

The music was banging hard, and the club was slapping. The dance floor was full, and it was packed up at the bar for people trying to get drinks. As they made their way to the VIP section, all eyes in the club were focused on them.

A red velvet rope separated VIP from the rest of the club. Two huge bouncers stood tall, working the rope. Recognizing Stackz, the red rope was immediately lifted, allowing him, Ava, and his entourage to walk through without question. Once everyone got settled in the booths, they began popping bottles and tossing back shots.

Hours passed. Everyone was feeling nice from the drinks and the cookie kush blunts that floated around the booths nonstop. Stackz and Ava were in their own world and had been all night. They danced together in VIP and whispered back and forth in each other's ear, talking freaky. Stackz promised a tipsy Ava that later on in the room, he was going to spend until daybreak "touching the bottom." Hearing him say shit like that was making her pussy wet and anxious to see if the big-dick rumors about him were indeed true. As the perfect night was drawing to a close, the bartender announced last call. Ordering one more bottle for the road, they all had a final drink before heading toward the exit of the club.

CHAPTER SEVENTEEN

Outside the club, the streets were packed with people going to their cars, trying to get to their next destination, either the casino or the nearest White Castle. Not wanting to go home alone, guys were getting at females in the parking lot, trying to get some intoxicated pussy to warm their beds until daybreak. Across the street from Detroit Live, Rank and Mickey were parked, posted, with murder on their unsettled minds. The revenge-driven pair had been sitting there all night smoking blunts and popping E-pills, waiting in hopes to see Stackz, Devin's killer. With their guns in their laps, Rank asked Mickey if he was ready. The answer was evident as Mickey slow stoked his pistol as if it was a cat in heat.

Both high and focused on revenge, the effects of the pills had them clearly not thinking right. The original plan was just to go, sit, and watch Stackz; see how he moved and what he was truly about. Yet, no sooner than Rank saw their mark exit the club with Ava on his arm, he threw the plan out the window, instantly becoming enraged. Hurriedly, he snatched his gun off his lap, pulling back the top, putting a bullet in the chamber. Mickey followed suit doing the same. Ready to make some noise and the news, they watched Stackz and Ava talk to a small crew of several guys as they stood outside of what had to be Stackz's Range Rover.

"Look at this bullshit right here! This bitch fucking this nigga who murked our boy. Really, Ava? She wouldn't give me the pussy, but *him?* That's messed up." Mickey rambled on out loud as if Ava could really hear him from across the street inside of the car.

People that were in the parking lot and on the side street were looking at the car Rank and Mickey were sitting in. Not used to going on missions without Devin there to instruct them on not being seen or heard, they were drawing way too much attention to themselves. T. L. noticed people looking in the direction of their car and got on high alert. Peering through the driver's side window, T. L. easily recognized Rank and Mickey from his own low-key, much-better-executed stakeout.

Easing over to Stackz's side, T. L. put him up on game, urging him to break out and leave the rest to him and the fellas. Ava peeped the mood change in Stackz, as well as everyone else standing around them. Asking if everything was good, Stackz assured her it was. He had no intentions to alarm her. He'd waited weeks to get the perfect pussy he'd seen in the hallway and wasn't going to let having to kill two nothing-ass niggas get in his way.

"Naw, it's all good this way. Just some loose-end business on the floor that needs to be picked up. Let's just head out and go get our room for the night. You hungry? You want something to eat?" Stackz played it off, not yet knowing where Ava's loyalties lay.

Making sure his date got in the truck, Stackz, being the gentleman that he was, shut Ava's door for her. After saying a few more things to T. L. and Gee, he jumped in the truck as well. Busting a quick suicide U-turn in the middle of traffic, they hit a side street, and then made a right turn toward Jefferson Avenue. When he and Ava came to a red light, they heard a bevy of gunshots in the same direction they'd just left.

Ava looked back over her shoulder, down the block, trying to see what she could. "Oh my God, Stackz, I know you heard them gunshots."

"Shawty, you safe; we both good, and that's all that matters right about now," Stackz replied, mashing the gas damn near to the floor. That gangster shit drama only made his dick rock hard. Headed to grab them a room for the night, he intended on giving Ava some serious pipe that would change her life.

It was pure pandemonium outside of Detroit Live as soon as Stackz and Ava were well out of harm's way. Rank and Mickey instantaneously drew all eyes on them. Almost to their demise, they let emotions get in the way of sticking to the game plan and got caught slipping in their feelings. Only if they could have controlled their high, then they could have seen who and what they wanted to and went on about their way. They could have holed up somewhere in a spot and made some plan of attack on their newly sworn enemy: Stackz. But that was too much like right, and they were under direct attack.

This was the moment T. L. had been waiting for and had no intentions of holding them up. Not once caring about the multitudes of soon-to-be witnesses that were innocently standing around, he reached back in the small of his waist, pulling out his twin sisters. With two nine's full-arm extended, T. L. let off round after round, gunning at his targets with intent to commit murder. Gee pulled out his gun and joined in on the assault.

As the ear-shattering sound of gunshots rang out, everyone start to scream, scatter, and try to take cover. Rank and Mickey wanted to get out of Dodge as well. They attempted to fire back but knew they had no win. Rank knew they weren't going to live if he didn't get them the fuck on. Trying to hold them off, he emptied his clip and dropped his gun down on the floorboard. He held his head tucked down, praying for Allah to help him get

Mickey and himself home safely. Rank fumbled with the key trying to put it in the ignition. With the car taking hit after hit, it rocked from side to side . . . ironically, the same way they'd done Stackz's beloved Jeep a few weeks back.

Blessed Rank finally turned the ignition over, starting the car. Under fire, he stayed low while yanking down the gear into drive. Slamming his foot down on the gas pedal as far as it would go, he recklessly hard whipped the steering wheel to the far right. "Stay down, my nigga," he yelled to Mickey. "We outta this bitch!"

Sideswiping a few parked cars on his getaway bid, he struck a terrified female trying to get to her car; collateral damage. As Rank cut the corner, he ran into another parked car with some nosey-ass dudes in it watching everything go down as they smoked a blunt. After hitting them, he almost lost control, but straightened up and got the fuck on.

Not even attempting to shoot back, Mickey was cowardly balled up halfway between the seat and the floorboard. He'd already pissed on himself after the first round hit the back door and had zoned out. "Get us the hell out of here, man; drive, drive, oh shit! Drive!" Shaking, he kept thinking about the night he'd taken the two slugs in the shoulder and knew he didn't want to feel that burning pain sensation now, again, or ever.

Rank drove the car off the main streets in case the police had a description of the car they were in. Still rattled, they gathered themselves together. After making sure they weren't hit, Mickey and Rank went back and forth, trying to figure out how Stackz's people knew who they were. They knew Ava didn't have an opportunity to see them from where she was standing, and Leela was on their team. It didn't take them long to both come to the same conclusion. At this point in the deadly game, it really didn't matter how they knew who they were. Now it was all about who kills who first.

Back at the club, Gee and T .L. told the bouncer as much as he needed to know so he could cover his ass when the police showed up. Jumping in their rides before the fingers started being pointed out to the law, Gee and T. L. agreed to get together by noon the next day to talk about how to handle these clowns that were so brave to try to lay on them and Stackz tonight.

CHAPTER EIGHTEEN

Stackz felt it was getting warm. Feeling the need to take his shirt off, he got it over his head and sensed Ava moving toward him. He felt her soft hands touching his abs, then trailing down to his waistband. He wasted no time hanging his shirt up on a hanger. Instead, he tossed it on the king-size bed and flexed his chest so it was jumping up and down.

Ava made a pleasing moan while watching him showing off. "Boy, I think that is so fucking sexy. Do it again for me."

Stackz smiled with a smirk and complied. "Like this?"

"Yeah, Stackz; just like that."

Stackz took his shoes off next, setting them in the corner of the room out of the way.

"Dang, I see you coming all out of your clothes and whatnot. I need to get a little comfortable myself. I'll be right back."

Stackz waited patiently for Ava to come out of the bathroom. He sat down on the bed and lay back on his elbows. After a short while, his bae returned. To his satisfaction, she blessed him by only having on a bra and panties. He'd seen her totally naked in the hallway of her house and had even held her nude body when she was struggling to get away, but this sight was so much different and alluring. Maybe it was the way the bra held her breasts close together and at full attention or the contour cut of the lace around her ass cheeks. Whatever it was, Stackz couldn't stop smiling as he was all in.

"Well, what you think?" she asked, spinning around for his approval.

Stackz shook his head and tried to resist jumping up and taking the pussy where she stood. "Trust me when I tell you, it's all good this way, ma; all good."

Ava came and sat on the bed. Leaning backward, she rested her back against the headboard. The two talked about the things they like to do more in-depth than when they talked on the phone, but not like this; up close and definitely about to become personal.

As it seemed to be confession time, Ava told Stackz she liked to go out with her friends on weekends, drink strawberry daiquiris, and just enjoy life in general when she wasn't in school. Stackz, being nosey, asked her how she paid for her classes.

After pausing briefly, she replied, "If I tell you, you might think less of me." She looked away as if what she did for a side hustle was in any way close to the madness that Stackz was off into.

"Look, I'm very open-minded, baby. Sometimes we do things in this crazy-ass life that we don't like to do, to better ourselves in the long run. Especially if we trying to make it out of the hood. You feel me? So keep it a hundred with me, and I'll do the same with you; today, tomorrow and always." His speech put Ava at ease.

"Okay, bae. Well, you already know I work at the doctor's office, right?"

"Yeah . . ."

"Well, I kinda run scripts there; unauthorized scripts. I only try to hustle them when I have to pay for my studies or maybe some extra books."

Stackz was quick to comply, not wanting to ruin the moment. "Okay, then. That ain't nothing major or something a guy like me can't handle. Like I just said, you gotta do what you gotta do in this world to get by."

Ava smiled, letting her defensive guard back down in the dimly lit room, "Thank you, Stackz, for not looking at me sideways. I appreciate that; for real."

"You mean the same way you could look at me after all the bullshit you know for a fact I done did? Dig this, Ava, I like what I see and what I'm hearing from you. You're smart and beautiful. Plus, I feel like I've known you for a long time; like I've met you before."

"I know, right? Strangely enough, I feel the same way, believe it or not." Out of nowhere, Ava changed the subject, feeling shit was getting too deep for what she truly had on her mind. "I know this is off track, but all night I've been admiring your lips. Can you kiss, Stackz?"

Making the first move after Ava brought the question up, Stackz sat facing her. "Come find out." Reaching for her chin, he tilted her head up to meet his lips. Kissing slow and passionate, their tongues danced in and out of each other's mouth.

Stackz's dick bricked up in his jeans attempting to burst free of its denim imprisonment. He held Ava close and their skin touched each other's. Stackz felt Ava's body grow warmer by the minute in his arms. Her kiss was intoxicating, and he wanted more as she slowly broke from their embrace. "Ava, can I have you?"

Immediately, Ava replied with her eyes closed in a sexy, whispering voice, "You already had me; since day one."

As she sat back, Stackz kept his eyes focused on hers. "Can I lay my head in your lap?"

Ava nodded, bringing his head down onto her lap. With lust in her heart, she began rubbing his thick, brushed waves. She slowly stoked his head in soft circular motions while tracing the outline of his face with her finger. Before Stackz knew what he was doing, he was biting her camel toe. Ava didn't stop him, even though she jumped. He kept at it, causing her to shiver from his biting and pulling at the material with his teeth.

Stackz's mind was shouting, *Nigga, fuck her good! Fuck her until she taps out!* With his head in her lap, he looked up at Ava and before he knew it, said in a low, deep, seductive tone. "Can I eat your pussy?"

Hearing the answer was a quick yes, Stackz leaned up, snatching Ava's body down the bed and flipped her over, all in one, strong-arm motion. He kissed the back of her neck and licked and sucked her earlobes. Ava's moans filled with excitement and anticipation turned him on. With the edge of the blanket balled up in her fist, pulling at them, Ava raised her ass tooted slightly up in the air as if begging Stackz to take her panties off. Moaning in a low tone, she wiggled her body around in a crawling motion, not going anywhere.

Stackz began slightly sweating, and his dick started to throb uncontrollably. Grabbing her by the ankles, he flipped her back over. Not being able to resist any longer, he finally eased Ava's panties down her legs. As they reached her painted pretty toes and feet, she opened her legs wide, allowing Stackz to finish taking the lace undergarment off. Tossing them to the chair on the side of the bed, he began massaging her feet, then her calves, then her thighs, until he reached her perfectly shaved kitty. As her body started to squirm, she turned her head, pressing the side of her face into the pillow.

Ava's moans had Stackz on edge. He was wanting to fuck her even more but knew it wasn't time. He knew he had to fuck her brains out, but not just yet; instead, he dry humped her, pressing his rock-hard manhood into her midsection so she could see what he was working with.

Stackz began to slip one finger, then two, inside of her hot, slippery, tight pussy. Ava's body jerked as he explored her inner sanctuary, and the wetness dripped from his touch. He slowly began licking and sucking the pussy juice that had run down her thigh to the back of her knees. Stackz made sure to lick both places as Ava shook with pleasure.

Using both his thumbs, Stackz parted her pussy wide, and began going to work. Opening his mouth wide, he unleashed his tongue deep into her shaven hole. He flicked his tongue up and down inside of her, tasting her wet walls. Ava attempted to run from Stackz, but he held her hips and continued eating her out. Focusing on Ava's clit, he stuck the tip of his tongue to it and started massaging it gently. After a few seconds of that, Ava was on the edge of the cliff and suddenly jumped off. Squirting come out of her tight little pussy into Stackz mouth, like the true freak he was, Stackz swallowed as much as we could while still sucking her pussy lips until she collapsed in ecstasy.

Stackz got up to wash his face. When he came back, he had a warm rag in his hand and placed it between Ava's legs. As he washed her up, she smiled.

"I get it now why bitches keep your name in their mouths," she smirked, watching his every move. When he turned to go wet the rag once more, she noticed a huge tattoo across his back but couldn't make out what it said. "Hey, bae, what does that tat on your back say?"

Stackz return to the bedside, hot rag in hand. Sitting down on the edge of the bed, he slightly lowered his head so Ava could take in all his jailhouse artwork. Rising up, with both of her soft hands, Ava ran them over the shoulder to shoulder black-colored words and read the words aloud: 100% GANGSTER.

"Every day," Stackz proudly stood to his feet turning around to face his queen. "Every fucking day!"

"Oh, it's like that," she smiled, knowing she finally had a real man ready to lead the way, not one of the suckers she'd been with in the past.

Stackz bent over, washing her cat once more. "Listen, Ava, want for nothing, ma, 'cause I got you. From this point on, no matter what jumps, I got you! We good!"

"Stackz, please don't get me twisted! I'm not a ho like my sister. I don't do this shit on the regular, I swear. I haven't been with a man in an entire year and hadn't wanted to until I met you. There's just something about you that I can't resist."

"Baby girl, I'm feeling you just the same. I can't explain it with words either, but I can show you." Throwing the wet rag onto the floor, Stackz climbed on top of Ava, positioning himself so he could enter her hot, wet pussy. Her mouth opened wide, her back slightly arched, and she looked as if she wanted to scream, and it wouldn't come out of her mouth as he slowly stabbed her with his dick. There was no feeling like the first time when a nigga slide dick up into new pussy. They both jointly wanted to remember the sensational feeling. Ava's pussy was just as tight as he thought it would be. And his dick was just as hard as she imagined. They both knew this night was just the beginning of something deeper than sex.

CHAPTER NINETEEN

Stackz dropped Ava off at home early the next morning. They had been up all night fucking hard and confessing all their sins. Ava got out of the truck feeling as if her life had changed for the better. Walking up the stairs and into the house, she was on cloud nine. Flashing back at the blissful time she had out at the club and at the room with Stackz, Ava didn't believe things could get any better. She showered and lay in her bed. Closing her eyes, she was thankful it was the weekend. Because if it wasn't, she wouldn't be going to work or class the way Stackz had dicked her down. Not accustomed to the way he'd stretched her legs and pounded her cat, Ava need at least twenty-four hours to recover. Gripping her pussy tight, she thought about Stackz's touch as she fell asleep.

Ava was dreaming that Stackz was fucking her hard doggie style. Her pussy was wet and throbbing. She was on the verge of climaxing when she was awaked by her sister Leela.

"Bitch, wake up! Get up, Ava, wake up." Leela was talking fast and loud, as if the house was on fire.

Ava snapped out of her wet dream and jumped out of the bed. Half asleep and sore, she was hotter than fish grease. "What the hell is wrong with you, girl? Why you up here fucking with me? Take your loud ass downstairs! You get on my damn nerves." Ava rubbed the sleep out of the corner of her eyes, promising to lock the basement door that joined the two levels.

"Forget all that! Ava, what the hell happened last night at the club? I just saw on the news a shootout took place at Detroit Live while the club was letting out. Were you there? Who got shot? They said a girl got hit by a car fleeing the scene." Leela bombarded her with question after question. "I know you was there, and I know you got the gossip. So what's the deal?"

"Look, you nosey bitch, I don't know what happen. We heard gunshots when we got to Jefferson Avenue, but ain't go back to see what jumped." Ava yawned as the bed commanded her to lie back down. "This is the first I'm hearing about any of what you talking about."

What Leela was really doing was covering her ass in case it came out that she told Rank and Mickey where Ava and Stackz would be last night. She knew Stackz and his brother, along with T. L., didn't play no games. And if she could keep her name from ringing with dirt and still avenge Devin's death, then why not try it? "Girl, I'm glad you okay. I was worried sick about you. What time did you get in? Did he give you some money?"

"Money? Girl, what the fuck you talking about? Why everything gotta be about money all the time with you? It's other things in the world besides money!"

Leela took two steps back, looking her sister up and down. "Oh yeah, like what?"

After they both laughed, Ava told her Stackz dropped her off a little after six this morning. Then she went on to tell Leela how good of a time he'd showed her and his entire crew. Ava lastly bragged to her how thirsty bitches were trying to get at Stackz and how he played them to the left.

Leela was low-key hating; wishing Ava had got shot and killed so she wouldn't have to deal with her any longer. Well, maybe not killed, but at least shot so she'd temporarily shut the fuck up with acting so stomach sick in love with Devin's killer.

"Well, I'm going back to sleep." Ava fluffed her pillow ready to make it her BFF.

Leela, low key, was glad their fake conversation was over. No longer interested in hearing about how good of a time she had last night anyhow, she rubbed her stomach thinking about how much she wanted the man who murdered her baby daddy dead. *I swear I hate Stackz and this backstabbing bitch for riding with his ass! I guess blood don't trump dick these days!*

Rank and Mickey were on the other side of town holed up in a bando. It was Mickey's grandmother house at one point but not anymore. It had been vacant for over three months now since the elderly woman lost it due to the taxes being delinquent. After the bank had boarded the single dwelling up, Mickey tore the wood barriers off the back of the house, reclaiming his family home. Needing a place to lie low at after the blotched shootout, this was the best place possible for them to be. They knew Stackz and his people would be on their trail, so staying on the East Side was out of the question.

Mickey had been thinking. Something about last night didn't seem right; didn't add up. He knew Leela was known to be grimy at times, and since Devin was gone, she really didn't have any true loyalty to him or Rank. Running down how he felt to Rank, he soon discovered he had been thinking the same exact thing. Leela was a snake. It just seemed so convenient to them both that Stackz would be waiting on them outside the club. Wasting no more time with speculation, Rank placed the call.

Leela answered her cell on the first ring, asking Rank right off rip, "Damn, what happened?"

Rank yelled into the phone, getting it real, "Bitch, you set us up! They was ready for us. That's what the fuck happened! Don't act stupid!"

"What the hell! Fuck outta here, nigga. No, I didn't set y'all up! Why the fuck would I do that dumb shit?"

"I dunno. *You* tell me why you'd do some ole ho shit like that! We over here both fucking wondering that! Please enlighten us!"

Leela was already heated with having to hear her sister's fairy-tale night with that wannabe hood Prince Charming and knew these busters wanna try to get on her head. Flat out, she wasn't trying to hear whatever they were claiming. "Listen, Rank, I want that punk that killed my baby daddy dead probably more than you and Mickey's good cosigning. I don't fuck with Stackz on no type of level, even though he giving my little sister the dick. So you can kill that dumb shit that's coming outta your mouth."

Still rolling off the E-pills he'd taken a few hours back, Rank tried to make sense of what Leela was saying. It started to sound convincing to him . . . or maybe he was just high; he couldn't decide.

Mickey, also still buzzing as well, was in the background yelling out this and that. "Yo, she lying, bro. She rolling with them niggaz. You know how these bitches be out here; bitter as fuck. That probably ain't even my manz baby her ass claim she knocked up with."

Leela was irritated that Mickey was trying to go on her and had her own set of lethal words to equally match his. "Listen, Rank, you can tell Devin's old hand puppet he can fall all the way back with moving that mouth of his. Tell him his puppet master is gone, so he can move around freely without the next nigga's hand up his ass telling him how to eat, shit, and sleep. Ole hating-ass bitch! Nigga just mad my sister ain't never wanna give him the pussy! Fuck him and fuck you too if y'all think I'd spit on Devin's memory like that!"

Rank was starting to get a massive headache. In between Leela and Mickey shouting in each of his ears, they had blown his high. Finally convinced she may be telling the truth, Rank begged Mickey to chill out. Then he told Leela he had to go handle some business and he'd be in touch in a few days. When Leela asked Rank where they were holding out at, he barked at her, telling her she didn't need to know all that, just in case he was wrong, then hung up the phone.

Stackz, Gee, and T. L. met up and talked about the next moves to be made. Stackz informed them to have everybody looking for Rank and Mickey. He wanted to deal with them quickly before shit got too out of hand to control that money can't make go away. He gave T. L. the green light to do what he does best.

T. L. was in a zone . . . finally being able to snap the chain Stackz had on him from killing up some shit. Stackz reminded them the money doesn't stop, so they don't stop getting it; still business as usual.

CHAPTER TWENTY

Three long grueling weeks had passed since Devin got his face shot half off by Stackz. After selling chicken and fish dinners and dry begging everyone they knew, Devin's family had finally put enough money together to lay him to rest. Today is the day. Thursday from 1:00 p.m. to 2:00 p.m. services will be held for Devin James Boyd at Swanson Funeral Home on Mack Avenue and East Grand Boulevard.

Rank and Mickey had been in hiding since the shit popped off at the club, but today, they agreed to chance their lives to pay their last respects to their fallen home-boy. They'd convinced Leela into going and pay her last respects to Devin as well, seeing that she claimed to be carrying his child. Of course, Leela wanted to attend to say her final farewells but knew her presence would not be a good idea. She'd already sprung for a floral arrangement to be sent and that was all she was willing to sacrifice, knowing, in reality, Devin wouldn't be around no more to bless her with money here and there after he hit a lick or caught some dope dealer slipping. Leela knew she was on her own also when it came to having his baby. After all, it took his broke-ass family three weeks to scrape up on funeral fare, so asking for milk and diapers would be out of the question.

After some coaxing from Rank and Mickey, Leela finally agreed as long as they promised that they would stand by her when she tells his family about the baby.

And not let Devin's crazy still-out-for-blood-holding-a-grudge sister jump on her. The mournful pair assured her that they would, as long as they both could be godfather to Devin's baby. Wanting all the potential financial help she could get, Leela agreed.

It was a little after 1:00 p.m. and the service had started for Devin Boyd. Having been left with half a face, the known setup individual had a closed casket service. The family couldn't afford to pay for the best reconstruction specialist, and even if they could, unfortunately, Stackz didn't leave them much in the way to work with.

Upon hearing of his victim's state, Stackz made insensitive jokes about Devin having to have a closed casket. He said, "All the king's horses and all the king's men couldn't put Devin's face back together again." T. L. and Gee thought it was funny, but Stackz would never say anything that ugly to Ava, let alone in ear range of Leela.

Rank, Mickey, and Leela arrived at the funeral home. After parking, they rushed inside the building. Quickly finding the room Devin's services were held in, Leela felt as if she was going to pass out or throw up. All three of them were unnerved. Mickey and Rank was looking for the unexpected killer to stand up in the middle the services and start shooting at them in retaliation for the attempt on Stackz's life, while Leela was afraid Devin's family wasn't going to be reasonable with her even being there; at least, his vindictive sister, for that matter.

Once the frightened trio entered the quiet room, everyone looked up to see who was coming in except for Devin's mother, sister, and aunt. They were sitting in the front row where no one really ever wanted to be. This was the time the best seats in the house weren't up front center. Some of Devin's people were grieving hard, bawling their eyes out about him dying so young, while others were whispering that they knew this bullshit was gonna happen considering the street lifestyle he led. Sad church music played low throughout the room as the three of them got their courage up to approach the bronze and sky-blue-colored casket which had a huge black-and-white picture of Devin sitting near it on a pedestal.

"Damn, closed casket. Man, look at this picture of him they used, all dressed up going to the comedy concert downtown last year. I remember that picture from off this Facebook page," Rank nudged Mickey, speaking in a low tone. "This shit is so messed up. I can't believe Devin up in that mug dead; gone."

Although Devin had been dead and gone weeks ago, this day, this time, seeing his picture alone beside a closed casket made the bullshit seemed like it just happened a few hours ago. It was like scraping the scab off a slow-healing wound.

This picture is terrible. Out of all the ones they could've used, why in the fuck did they pick this one? Tears flowed like a water facet turned on full blast from Leela's red eyes as she stared at the photo of Devin. She couldn't help but think about the last time she saw him on the restaurant floor looking so pitiful at her as she stepped over him like he was no more than a mere piece of garbage.

Rank held back tears. He cautiously scanned the room for anyone that looked like they didn't belong. Paranoid, he was ready to shoot it out inside the funeral home and risk killing anyone that got in his way if he had to, including Devin's grieving mother. He, just like Mickey and even Leela, didn't want any trouble. Like everyone else that was hopefully there, they just wanted to pay their final respects and go home. Huddled together as if they were connected at the hip, they walked up the middle aisleway. Moving closer toward the casket and the front of the room to offer their condolences to the family, Devin's sister lifted her face that had been buried in her hands when Mickey reached over, placing his hand gently on her shoulder. No sooner than she turned her head around, she looked on the other side of Mickey and locked eyes with Leela. As if on cue—all hell broke loose.

Leaping to her feet, Devin's already mentally distraught and drained sister went berserk and had to be physically restrained. She couldn't believe that after all that had been said and done over the past few weeks since her brother's death that Leela had the bad taste to actually show up. That she had the nerve, the balls, the guts, to march right up to her deceased brother's casket like she was his loyal wifey or some shit like that.

"Get her out of here! Your ass not welcome in here! Bitch, it's your fault Devin lying up in a casket now in the first place; running around trying to impress your high yellow ugly ass!"

"Really?" Leela slowly spoke looking at Devin's sister, praying she didn't have to reach in her purse and pull out the double-edged butcher knife she brought with her just in case Mickey and Rank wouldn't or couldn't do as they promised. Taking her chances, Leela didn't flinch or move; she stood her ground. Right then and there, she decided if anyone deserved to be standing at the right side of Devin's casket, it would be her; his soon-to-be baby momma.

Rank and Mickey moved in front of Leela with their hands up, pleading with Devin's sister to calm down and just hear what Leela had to say. The older aunt reined Devin's sister temporarily back in line, quickly becoming the sole voice of reason. Hoping to diffuse the explosive situation, she expressed to everyone that this isn't the time or place for this type of nonsense.

Leela didn't want any trouble and tried to let Devin's enraged sister know just that. Still in tears, she went on to explain to his entire family she was having his baby; his seed; his firstborn, meaning his only born. Leela told his mother that she'd carry on Devin's memory with his child and wanted them to be a part of the baby's life as well. Their involvement in Devin Jr. or little Devina's life was totally up to them.

Mumbling amongst the family and friends in the funeral moved around like a tidal wave. Caught off guard, no one knew what to say or what to do. They were speechless at Leela for dropping her newborn love-child bomb. After a short speech about the true meaning of family, the aunt painstakingly got everybody on the same page, reluctantly, to accept Leela and the glimmer of light out of this dark day. With her head still containing several staples, thanks to Ava, Devin's sister didn't care what her aunt said or this bitch claimed. She knew Leela was nothing but a whore and a liar.

All the while the confusion was taking place, Mickey and Rank kept searching the small crowd fearing possible retribution. Spooked, they felt like they had been exposed too long out of hiding. They were still doing E-pills that had the two of them paranoid. Rank and Mickey informed Leela they had to get off the street; it wasn't safe for them to be out like that exposed. Then they slipped out the rear exit so as not to be seen by anybody that might be looking for the infamous pair.

Leela had made it home from the funeral and was having mixed emotions. She felt relieved that she'd gotten somewhat of an understanding with Devin's family about her having his baby. Already having three kids whose fathers or their families were not around, Leela, deep down inside, truly didn't give a fuck about Devin's people either, but welcomed their help, if any, with the baby when he or she was born.

Ava's friend's car was parked out front of the house. Leela hated her, because she always thought she was better than everybody else. She was worse than Ava on that tip, if that was at all possible. Just to be spiteful, Leela took her house keys out of her purse and walked up on the girl's car. Having no concern or remorse, she dragged her key along the side of the car causing a deep long scratch.

After doing her dirt, Leela tiptoed up to Ava's, just to be nosey. She moved quietly, so as not to be heard. She peeked around the corner and didn't see them in the front room. Hearing voices coming from the back, Leela eased down the hall toward Ava's bedroom. Getting closer, she could hear them gossiping about Ava and Stackz's night out and how good he'd fucked her and how she was really feeling him.

Leela was heated to hear her blood be so two-faced. As she held her belly looking down, Leela swore she'd make Stackz pay as well as Ava. *Fuck her and that murderer; he gon' pay for killing my baby daddy.* Needing to throw up, Leela crept back downstairs as quietly as she'd come up.

CHAPTER TWENTY-ONE

Stackz and Gee sat in the driveway waiting on a phone call to go pick up money they were due. They agreed a long time ago how they would conduct their business and govern themselves in the streets. No re-up money; no bag, no shorts, or I-owe-this-much excuses. Stackz wasn't playing around about his money; never had and never would. He understood that this life they were living was not promised. He'd spent enough time locked behind bars to know, in a drop of a dime, shit could go from a nigga sitting real right . . . to him being down on his luck with his knuckles scraping the ground. Not only had he seen it happen firsthand to some of his direct competitors but heard thousands of tragic stories from dudes giving time to the prison just like him.

The serious subject changed from getting money, making money, and keeping money, to Gee expressing to Stackz bad vibes he was feeling about him dealing with Ava. It didn't sit well with Gee that Stackz was in as deep with Ava as he was. He advised his big brother that he needed to cut her loose. After what had jumped off at the club, Gee felt, in the long run, Ava was like her sister, Leela; grimy and couldn't be trusted. He predicted he only saw more bullshit coming their way if Stackz kept fucking around with the manipulative she devil in high heels.

Not trying to hear what Gee was saying in the way of leaving Ava alone, he told him to mind his own business;

he had his personal relationship with the "she devil" under total control. Stackz then reminded Gee that he should be worried about finding the two clowns that needed to be dealt with and leave his pussy problems to him.

Gee assured him he was on it and their time running around town like they'd done no wrong was soon coming to an end. He exposed he had gotten word earlier today that they may have been hiding out somewhere across town. One of his people shot him a text saying that the two MIA small-time thugs had been spotted at the funeral home where Gee and Stackz thought they may have showed up at to see their fallen comrade. Gee also mentioned that Leela was also seen going in the funeral home with them to say her final farewells to one of her fuck buddies.

Stackz rubbed his chin and nodded his head, satisfied their low-level reign of terror on the unsuspecting would be thwarted.

"Yeah, bro, real talk. I knew Leela was probably gonna go to ole boy hookup and whatnot, but she still been on some other shit lately." Gee put Stackz up on game that Leela had been acting funny toward him over the past few weeks, and he didn't trust her anymore. Trying to put all the pieces together before he reacted, Gee wanted to find out if Leela knew where they were going to the night of the shootout. Because, as he stated the night the shit had popped off, it wasn't any random coincidence they just "happen" to be at the club the same night at the same time.

Stackz felt the same as his baby brother. Something just wasn't right. Without hesitation, he let Gee know he would ask Ava later on tonight when they got together.

"Get together? Again? Tonight? Man, what the fuck? Is you sprung? So, damn, she's your main bitch now or what?" Gee barked at his brother, not believing Stackz was turning his player's card in. "Next thing next, your ass gonna be trading in the Range for a station wagon."

"It is what it is, nigga; ain't no secret," Stackz popped right back at him with a huge grin on his face.

Later that evening after Stackz got his business in order he headed home. Blessed to make it back to his crib and out of the mean streets, he took a deep breath and thanked God. He loved his line of work, because after five o'clock, no later than six at the first of each month, his work day was over. That was the beauty of trapping heroin; you set your business hours and when it's over, it's over; fuck it, it's over. His clientele knew to get all they needed to get them through the night because it was mad crazy dangerous after dark trying to chase that dragon.

Stackz hated it when he used to sell crack. He had to work three times as hard and stay up for days on end—make what in one week what he makes now in one day. After counting up all the money his team got out of the mud today, Stackz rubber banded it all up in thousand-dollar racks. Moving the dining-room table over, he then placed the money in the floor safe he'd had specially built. No one knew where this safe was at; not even Gee. Stackz knew that if he ever died out in the streets, the new owner of his house would be blessed if and when they ever decided to get new carpet.

After calming himself down from the day, Stackz took a long, hot shower. Preparing a fruit smoothie, he grabbed a protein bar as well and caught the tail end of the news. An hour later, he called Ava telling her he would be by to pick her up shortly because they needed to talk. With a raised eyebrow, Ava wanted to know exactly about what;

however, Stackz told her she'd find out when he picked her up; just be ready.

Ava hung up the phone and was puzzled about what it could be. She'd noticed something in the way he said, *just be ready*. That bothered her.

Stackz picked Ava up like he said he would. They sat at an upscale bar and grill to eat and have a few drinks. After awhile of talking about this and that, Ava finally cut off into him. She knew something wasn't right with him. She could tell he had something on his mind because he wasn't himself.

"Okay, dang, bae, what's wrong?"

"Just one thing in particular, Ava." Stackz, like her, went right to it. He got straight to the point. He wasn't going to let no good pussy blind him or get him off his square. "Okay, it's like this. Somebody told those niggas where we would be the night we all went out. I mean, on some real shit, you think outta all the places in the city, they just stumbled up on us and Gee? Just on the damn humble?"

Ava pushed her empty glass to the middle of the table and looked at Stackz questioning. Then asked him what he was trying to say . . . that she told them where they would be that night? "Hold the fuck up. I know you ain't trying to say I told them nothing-ass bums to come shoot not only you up but my black ass too! Is *that* what the fuck you saying?" Her voice grew louder with each passing word.

Stackz told her he wasn't saying she did it and to calm down. He knew she was official. However, then he asked her the million-dollar question, and that was . . . Did she tell her sister. Ava put her hand over her mouth. It now all made sense to her. Her eyes narrowed as she looked in Stackz's eyes confessing that she had indeed told Leela where she was going that evening. "That bitch asked me where the turnup was that night right before you picked me up. And I swear to God, I never thought about it or put two and two together that that trick would be so messy!"

"So that explains it then." Stackz finished his drink, needing another.

Ava knew she and Leela went at it constantly and had been since childhood, but this was beyond a fight over borrowing each other's clothes or lipstick. This was unimaginable. Ava couldn't believe her sister would put her directly in harm's way. "I would be lying if I said she wouldn't do anything like that to maybe someone else, but the bitch knew I was gonna be with you and didn't care if I got shot—her own sister! She always been jealous and envious of me. She so damn petty. I ain't even tell you what she did with the flowers you sent me. That heffa threw 'em away!"

Stackz paused, then gave her a halfway smile. "What you mean threw them away?"

"Meaning, I came home from work and found the flowers, the box, and the note stuffed in the trash." Ava was in full confession mode, giving Stackz a glass insight on who she was when she got pissed and where her loyalties really lay. "I went in on her silly ass. I already told her she had to move outta my house 'cause she refused to get right. But now, trust, she gotta go tonight! Let's go. Pay the damn bill!"

Stackz shook his head in disgust at what he was hearing. Waving the waitress over, he told her he'd have another double shot of 1738 and to bring Ava another of the same she was drinking. "Chill out, okay?" he smiled. "Pump your brakes. Let's just drink these drinks and eat. She'll be there when you get home."

Ava was still pissed and not ready to let it go that easy. "Naw, Stackz, I'm tired of carrying that girl on my back, and she the damn oldest! She don't want jack shit for her or her kids. Matter of fact, me and my momma do more for her kids than she even think about. And the bitch was like fuck my life!"

Stackz got Ava to finally calm down. After a few more drinks and a good meal, she started to feel some sort of way realizing who she was with, and the fact that he didn't play no games. Cut nothing like her sister, Ava couldn't have a blatant disregard for Leela's life like Leela obviously had for hers. Maybe it was the liquor that had changed Ava's mind-set or maybe it just wasn't in her to be so callous, but whatever the case was, for her nieces' and nephew's sake, she spoke out.

Ava placed her hand over the top of Stackz's hand. With tears about to bubble over and fall down her face, she begged him not to kill her sister if he really cared about her. "Please, Stackz, please let her dumb ass live. I know what she did was fucked up, and she don't deserve another chance. And matter of fact, I don't wanna give her another chance to fuck over you or me either. Trust me, I'm gonna throw her fake ass out as soon as we get back. She's dead to me, I swear." She allowed her tears to drop as she pleaded her case. "It's just my mother and her damn kids would be hurt if her ass wasn't around no more. Period. Please, Stackz, for me!"

Stackz took everything she'd said in consideration and against his better judgment, he decided to let Leela live. He knew she was going to be trouble in the long run, and he would make sure she got hers one way or another, but just not directly by his hand. "On some real shit, Ava, I feel nothing for your sister; absolutely nothing. And you're the only reason Leela is still breathing right now, because I care about you. Now I know you just talking shit about her being dead to you, but you better watch yourself because one day, her good hating ass gonna mess and get you into some shit you can't cry y'all way out of. Remember, bae, being blood to motherfuckers nowadays don't mean shit."

And on that note, Stackz swore to Ava he'd keep this conversation between the two of them, because he wasn't the one she had to worry about killing her sister. Ava knew exactly what Stackz was saying; he could never tell Gee or especially T. L.

The ride back to Ava's house consisted of little to no conversation between the two. They both were in their own thoughts about the whole Leela situation and how it should be handled. Ava was beyond fed up with her sister's selfish ways. She had her mind made up. Leela had to go; not tomorrow, not next week, but tonight. Ava knew she wouldn't feel comfortable with her under her roof one more night after Leela's shadiness had been fully exposed.

Finally pulling up at Ava's, Stackz came to a complete stop. Reaching under his seat, he grabbed his gun and began scanning the block for anything or anybody out place. Ava sat in the passenger seat with her arms folded looking straight-ahead, trying to think of what to say to Stackz. She was in her feelings with him, and she was sure he was in his toward her. Ava didn't want to get out of the truck and leave things up in the air. Turning to Stackz, she told him with no hesitation that she wanted to be with him. And if she had to choose between him or Leela, she chose him. Stackz let his guard down for a moment as he looked at Ava and took in what she had just told him. Not having to say anything else, Ava got out of the truck and began to walk toward the porch. Stackz called out to her, and she looked back over her shoulder to see what he wanted.

"Bae, you sure you good?" he threw his hands up.

"Yeah, bae, I'm more than good," she replied, taking her house keys out of her purse. "'Cause we good!"

CHAPTER TWENTY-TWO

Leela was smoking a blunt, oblivious to the storm that was headed in her direction. She'd heard a car pull up in front of house and peeked outside because the weed had her paranoid. Seeing it was only Ava and Stackz sitting outside in his truck talking, she wanted to throw up. She was on fire with envy, wishing death on them both. Slow strolling to the door, Leela opened it when she saw Ava heading toward the house. Ava had already taken her keys out of her purse, but put them back when she saw the downstairs door.

Ava was determined to make things right with her and Stackz and call Leela out on all her antics; past and present. Walking in with a purpose, Ava brushed past Leela in the doorway, deliberately bumping her with her shoulder. She had no intentions to physically fight her older sister, but when she saw Leela standing there with a smug look on her face, Ava came close to losing it. She wanted nothing more than to ball up her fist and sock Leela dead in her mouth for what she'd attempted to do to Stackz and her that night. She could definitely understand Leela being mad at Stackz for killing Devin, but she was there at the restaurant just like her. And Leela knew good and damn well Devin bought his own one-way ticket to hell that night. Stackz was just minding his business, so for him defending himself and choosing to live instead of die, he was public enemy number one in her mind.

Not saying a word, Ava dropped her purse to the floor and began grabbing anything that wasn't nailed down belonging to Leela, hurling it toward the front door.

Leela protested, shouting at Ava, "What the hell are you doing throwing my stuff like that? Girl, have you lost your damn mind? What's this about?"

Ava's answer was short and sweet. "Bitch, you know what this is and what this is about." She never let up throwing Leela's world all into the front room. "I know you told Rank and Mickey where we would be that night. You tried to get me killed, right along with Stackz. You straight foul."

Of course, Leela denied it and began picking up her belongings with one hand while the blunt still burned in the other.

Ava told Leela she can't trust her being underneath her roof and won't carry her any more. "Naw, you can keep denying that bullshit all you want. I ain't stupid, and neither is Stackz! Your free ride on my back ends tonight."

"Oh, I see what this is about; this shit is about that murderer." Leela acted as if she was having an *aha!* moment.

"Naw, this is about you being just like your dead-ass boyfriend Devin; setting niggas up, crying foul when you get caught. Ole throw-a-rock-hide-your-hand-type of niggas!"

Having heard enough of her rotten-to-the-core sister keep talking slick and threatening Stackz and her lives, Ava physically pushed Leela out the door onto the front porch, but not before taking her house keys.

Leela was beyond pissed at her sister and the low-down stunt she'd just done. Carrying an armful of her belongings, she fumed thinking how she would get back at Ava for siding with Stackz and treating her like she was no more than some garbage that needed to be thrown away. Banging on their mother's front door, Leela couldn't believe they'd figured out it was her that had tipped off Rank and Mickey so easily and prayed Stackz would bring no real harm her way. She knew if the shoe was on the other foot and she'd found out that Ava had basically said fuck her getting shot on the humble, she'd probably react the same way. But the hell with that. Ava didn't even give her a chance to her grab her lotion, her extra stash of weed she knew she'd had no business even still smoking since finding out she was pregnant, or her toothbrush. Her little sister just came through the door going hard in the paint. The more Leela thought about the fight she'd just had with her sibling, the harder she beat on the door. Close to six minutes of standing on the porch waiting and looking stupid, Leela heard her mother talking loud from the other side of the locked door.

"Hey! Hey! Stop banging on my goddamn door. What's wrong with you?" her mother slurred, gone off a pint of Crown Royal.

"Damn, open the door, Ma, would you?" Leela yelled back with an inflated attitude while dropping some of her items out of her arms.

Fed up with her daughter's fire-hot mouth, Mrs. Westbrook snatched the door open and gave her a piece of her mind, half-drunk or not. She called Leela every name in the book except for a child of God. She knew she wasn't and maybe hadn't been the best mother in the world to her two girls, but as much as she continued to do for Leela, even though she was grown, Mrs. Westbrook was done kissing ass to keep the peace.

"You're not going to just keep coming around here when you want to, messing with these kids' minds. You don't show up at no parent-teacher meetings. You won't fill out the paperwork so the youngest can go to day care, and we both know you make me beg you practically every month for that damn benefit card so your damn babies can eat! I'm tired, Leela, I'm fucking tired!"

"Look, Ma, ain't nobody trying to hear all that bullshit tonight. It's late as hell, and your ass been drinking. Your daughter, that bitch Ava, put me out, so I need to crash here for a few days until I figure out what to do next."

"Na-uh, girl! You ain't staying in my damn house no more. Not after last time. I told you your kids could stay with me anytime 'cause I don't want my grandbabies exposed to your crazy lifestyle, but *you?* No; hell naw! So you can go on somewhere else with that stuff you carrying." She went on to preach that grown-ass women that had a working pussy, fucking God knows who, that's into she doesn't know what, shouldn't be broke. "And besides that, just what in the hell did you do to your sister to throw you out just like that anyhow?"

Of course, Leela didn't want to say. Not because she was ashamed, but because she didn't want to hear any more of her mother's cruel judgmental speeches. Quickly informed that she could wash her ass there, if need be, and eat a hot meal, Leela's mother laid down the law, telling her living up in her house again wasn't going to ever happen.

Leela's two oldest came from out of the back room half-asleep and saw their mother, who was still getting read the riot act by their grandmother. Both giving her a dry hello, they kept it moving. They were used to her not staying long when she'd stop by, so making a big deal about her presence was low on their list of things to celebrate.

Mrs. Westbrook was in rare form telling Leela she needed to get her shit together so she could take care of her own kids, because she's getting too old to be playing momma to her grandkids. Defiant and nonreceptive,

Leela was rocking back and forth as she stood against the door frame of the dining room. What her mother was saying went in one ear and out the other.

Now Leela was pissed at her mother as well. She asked her didn't she care if she had no place to stay or not? And in no uncertain terms, her mother flat-out replied no, she didn't care. And that she must have done or said something way over the top or out of order for her little sister to just put her out in the street in the middle of the night. "So, Leela, what was it? What in the hell did you do this damn time? With you, it's always something. Hell, I'm surprise she put up with your ass for as long as she did."

Leela snapped. She stayed silent long enough, hoping her mother would have some sort of mercy on her and let her stay, at least for the night. But she saw that wasn't going to happen and was tired of letting her run her rum-drunk mouth. "Damn, why in the fuck you always taking her side? I swear you don't never give a bitch a break!"

"A break? A fucking break? Are you serious? Have you lost your damn mind, girl? I give your ass a break all day, every day, when I keep these kids so you can run around in the streets behind all the niggas getting nothing but a wet pussy and more babies for me and Ava to take care of!"

"I swear, I hate both of y'all bitches. I wish y'all was dead!"

Her mother looked at her in such a way that if looks could kill, Leela herself would have dropped dead on the spot. Without saying another word, her mother went in the kitchen grabbing a butcher knife.

Knowing she'd opened her mouth one time too many times challenging her mother, Leela saw the blade pointed at her neck and knew her mom would use it. Opting not to press her luck and get sliced by her mother's drunken rage, Leela bolted through the front door and onto the porch. Out of her mother's house having no family or friends that would take her in, Leela called the only ones that had been riding with her since this nightmare started: Rank and Mickey. Out of loyalty to Devin, they agreed to pick Leela up and get her off the streets.

CHAPTER TWENTY-THREE

Three weeks had come and gone since Ava had confronted Leela, throwing her out onto the street. Neither she nor her mother had heard from Leela since that night. Proving their point that she didn't care anything about her kids, Leela at least could have called to check up on their well-being, but she didn't even bother to do that. Ava stopped by her mother's house almost every day and helped out with food, clothing, and giving her mom a break so that she could have time for herself; even if that did mean her having a drink to calm her nerves and supposedly "get her mind right." It was a hard job going back in time, having to raise three small children when all of your own were grown.

Ava and Stackz were good with their relationship. With not having to look over her back, not having to deal with random dudes, and not worrying about Leela being on-site to tell Mickey and Rank their every move, the couple was ecstatic. As far as Ava was concerned, Leela could stay ghost for good. Normally not one of those females that would choose a man over her family or friends, Leela's unpredictable, backstabbing, conniving, and I-don't-give-a-fuck-about-no-bitch-but-my-damn-self attitude made it way easy for Ava to turn into one. She and Stackz had grown closer, spending more and more time together thanks to Leela's absence, drama free.

***

Ava and Stackz were wrapped up underneath his bed-sheets in a deep sleep. The two had gone out together to a strip club where a few big-name rappers had performed and had a long and wild night. Like always, Stackz and his crew showed up and showed out, spending major money. Crazy as it was, the high-profile entertainers that night felt Stackz was stunting too hard on them, garnishing all the shine. Knowing they couldn't outdo a real boss in his own city, they sent him and Ava a couple of Gold bottles to his booth and rocked out with him in VIP.

Stackz was jarred from his slumbering dreams, waking up to a ringing iPhone that lay on the nightstand beside the bed. Fighting to open his eyes, he looked at the alarm clock. It was 7:23 a.m. It was much too early for his phone to be blowing up like that on a Sunday morning, so he knew it had to be either an emergency or some major business on the floor. Picking it up, he soon saw the number, realizing it was his brother Gee.

Now awake, Ava turned over, rubbing her hands across his back. "Is everything okay, bae? What time is it?"

"I don't know yet," he dry throat mumbled, answering his phone. "Hey, what'sup, dude? We still in the damn bed sleeping like a motherfucker."

On the other end of the line Gee was frantic as he excitedly revealed the nature of his early-morning inter-ruption to his brother's sleep. "Yo, my nigga, we got these ho-ass buster over here where I'm at right now! They about to be hit and hit hard!"

Stackz knew exactly who Gee was talking about, so no names had to be mentioned. "Oh yeah? And where is that?" he causally asked, not wanting Ava all up in his street affairs; especially considering . . .

Gee shouted the address into the phone, which Stackz committed to memory. Jumping out of bed, he moved fast getting dressed. Not knowing what was happening,

Ava jumped up as well, shadowing her man's every move, asking him questions about what was wrong and what was going on.

Stackz bossed up, demanding she stop with the questions and go back to bed and he'd be back in an hour or so. Wrapped in a sheet, as Ava watched him pull out of the driveway, she was both scared and confused, praying Leela was not involved.

CHAPTER TWENTY-FOUR

Stackz pulled up behind Gee's F-150. Getting out of his own ride, he then got into the truck with his brother. Gee was hell-bent on tying up all loose ends. He'd been out in the streets handling his business, making sure that would take place sooner than later. He had one of his young but anxious-to-please goons sitting in the backseat. Trained to go at any given moment, the criminal-minded youngster repeated to Stackz what he had already told to Gee.

"Yeah, so, I was dropping off one of my little jump offs and a nigga stopped at the gas station. You know I needed to get a swisher to roll up for my morning hookup, you feel me? And just like fucking that, I straight recognized that lame who can't aim right," he laughed, having a mental flashback.

"Can't aim right?" Stack repeated.

The boy continued telling his story as he checked to see if he had lost the red cigarette lighter he'd brought earlier, alone with the swisher. "Yeah, dude that couldn't aim or hit shit. That fag from the night at the club when we was banging at him. Dumb ass all stepping to me and had no fucking clue who the fuck I was."

Stackz was all in, realizing what he'd been hoping would jump with the pesky menaces could be within arm's reach. "Hell naw, are you sure it was that bitch?"

"Yo, I'm telling you it was him. Ho-ass nigga tried to sell me some reggie, acting like it was kush or some shit. I could tell that bag was garbage right off the rip 'cause I get down every day, you feel me?" The goon nodded his head wanting to blaze up right then and there. "But, of course, I played the role. I told him I only cop halfs at a time, 'cause anything less wouldn't make sense to a real smoker like me."

"Right, right." Gee threw his two cents in, cosigning what the boy was saying.

"Yeah, fake wannabe boss, no doubt ain't have what wanted to cop on him. So I showz the nigga the money, and he say, I got you. Dude say, 'Follow me around the block to my spot.'"

Stackz was all the way in. This was the day he'd been waiting for since the night back at the restaurant when he should have killed the other two assholes like he had they manz. "Say word! This nigga out here in these Detroit streets calling himself having a spot; rocking and rolling."

"That's what the fuck I said too, bro," Gee once again chimed in. "These fools out here calling themselves living life and shit like it ain't gonna be consequences to they bullshit!"

The young goon was feeling himself. Like a kid getting blessed at Christmas, Stackz and Gee were giving him nothing but praise on top of praise for the information he'd delivered. Slowly creeping, bending the corner, he proudly pointed the appearing-to-be-damn-near-unlivable so-called spot out.

"That's it right there; the one with the porch windows boarded up."

The house sat three deep off the corner. It looked like most dwellings in Detroit . . . good for trapping out of; a bando. Gee was more than willing to allow Stackz to take the lead. Asking him how he wanted to play the situation, he would happily fall in line with whatever move his older brother dictated they make. Stackz was seething, wanting nothing but for this entire bullshit to be put to bed. Announcing to Gee as well as their loyal soldier sitting in the rear of the truck it was time to nip this shit in the bud today, everyone agreed.

"We need to make sure we do this shit clean as possible. Ain't no need for one of us to fall or drop the ball on the humble. These cats ain't about that life—at all!"

After making sure they'd double whipped their bullets, each reloaded their clips. It was showtime, and in the minutes to soon follow, things were about to be all bad for any occupants of the house. Parked around the corner, they each got out of the truck. Checking the perimeter on the nearly deserted block, they headed toward the house via a few vacant lots. As they crossed through the last lot nearing their destination, the youngin' informed them when he was inside the house he only saw two guys and no one else; meaning, they had the fools outnumbered off jump. Having seen the way his soon-to-be victims reacted under pressure in the nightclub parking lot as well as how young dawg said they were taking potshots, he knew this shit should be easy as hell. Straight murder. In and out. Gee and Stackz stood off to the side, guns in hand, while the young goon knocked at the door.

Rank and Mickey sat posted in the front room with the radio on low just for some background noise. Exchanging pipe dream ideas about how they could become millionaires overnight instead of being the nickel-and-dime hustlers they were, they smoked a blunt. Mickey didn't smoke half as much as Rank but stayed more 'noid when he did. Sitting at a makeshift table made up of two plastic blue milk cartons and a piece of an old medicine cabinet door, Mickey sacked up a few ounces of reggie they'd mixed with kush. Taking turns being on the door, Mickey hated to be the one that actually put the bags of mixed trees he and Rank claimed were exotic bud in the hands of customers and take their money. When Devin was alive, he used to at least make sure they had some semi-decent product to move; even if he had to rob another drug dealer to get it. Now, Mickey was stuck following behind Rank, who had almost less sense than he did; only more guts to go for bad.

Rank was stretched out on the floor. Lying on top of a pile of old dirty blankets his grandmother left behind when she lost the house to foreclosure, he was good for the time being. Although he and Mickey weren't making as much cash as they could, at least it was something. They were on the come up, so they had to spend the least as possible and kick in the majority of the bread to re-up and rebuild. The more they copped, the lower the price would be, which, of course, in turn, meant more profit. Rank had just finished eating a cheeseburger deluxe and was watching Mickey bag up like a hawk. He knew his homeboy was soft and would fuck around and not mix some of the bags, claiming he hated to play people in their face. Mickey stayed, saying his mother said karma was his first cousin and like bad luck, would always be in their family's tainted bloodline.

After twenty minutes or so smoking and talking shit, there was a knock at the front door. Rank's stomach had been on bump since finishing that cheeseburger. Feeling it start to bubble once more, he held his side, informing Mickey it was his turn to get the door.

"Dawg, you get it and serve whoever. I gotta take a piss and get rid of some more of that damn food. I swear to God that shit meat must've been tainted." As he walked down the hallway to the bathroom, he saw Leela's whining-about-this-and-that ass curled up on an old box spring. Not wanting to wake her up and have to hear Leela talking shit about how much she hates her sister, despises her mother, can't stand her no-good kids, and so on, Rank pulled the door closed. Across the hall in the other bedroom his grandmother used to sleep in, he and Mickey's pit bull puppies were also curled up asleep. Only instead of an old box spring, it was a pile of dirty, mildewy, dog-piss-and-shit clothes the frisky pets had pulled out of the closet that they made their bed.

"Yeah? Who dat?" With his finger on the trigger, Mickey put bass in his voice, yelling through the door. Even though he and Rank were only selling weed and pills, times were hard in the city of Detroit. Desperate to make ends meet, every resident was searching for a come up and stayed mad at the world for being broke. Motherfuckers, no matter young or old, would kill a person for sneezing too loud in the middle of a movie if they saw fit. There was no limit or special treatment given; in the game or out or never have played—no passes; no exceptions. If you left yourself open to get got, then nine outta ten times, you were already as good as dead. It would only be a matter of time and trust; everyone got a turn.

Mickey asked again who was on the other side of the door as he gripped up more tightly on the handle of his pistol. He knew most of their clientele would hit them up to let him or Rank know they were on their way, but every so often, niggas would just pop up on the humble, knowing they were posted twenty-four-seven. "Yo, what up, doe? Who the fuck is it? What you need?"

"Hey, what up, doe? It me; dude from earlier from the gas station. I want to get another half right quick of that kush."

Mickey was still asking who was it again and what exactly they wanted at the same time he was dumbly taking the 2-by-4 from across the door that secured it.

He looked out of the small window on the door that was covered with a flimsy piece of cardboard. Easily, he recognized the guy from earlier that morning who'd copped. Rank and he both were jocking the fact dude had the new Jordans on days before they were due to drop. He'd promised them the hookup on his sneaker plug and didn't try to negotiate on their weed price or the play. So instantly, this guy they'd known less than a five-minute transaction had become a person Mickey believed that could be trusted.

Outside, Stackz, Gee, and the youngin's adrenalin was pumping fast and hard hearing the board being removed, meaning the deadbolt locks were next to follow. It would only be a matter of seconds before Stackz would avenge the attempt made on his life.

"Oh yeah, my dude with them Jordans. What up, doe?" Mickey still had his gun in his hand but had gotten too relaxed. Strike one, two, and three. As he was turning the knob, pulling the door open, the young goon pushed it with force, causing it to hit Mickey in the face. He was knocked off balance, almost falling to the floor. The youngster laughed that the caper was going as planned, immediately bolting inside, grabbing Mickey's hand with the gun. Stackz and Gee bum-rushed in right behind him, pointing their pistol around the living room searching for any other persons. Mickey and the youngin' struggled, but it was brief. Not wanting to get his hood-worshiped sneakers scuffled any further than need be, the youngster shot Mickey in his hip. High off the weed he'd smoked, Mickey was in a half-dazed fight-or-flight mode. He knew after taking a bullet to the hip, he couldn't take flight, so fight to survive it was. He yelled out for Rank to help him. However, Rank didn't respond. By that time, Stackz and Gee had run up into the main part of the house ready to disarm and destroy whoever else was there.

Gee covered the front rooms with his gun drawn while Stackz went toward the back. Gee checked every inch of the foul-smelling dwelling finding no one in the front. Returning to help the young soldier with Mickey, he helped drag him to dining room. As he bled from the lower-body gunshot wound, he started to panic like he had when he took the two slugs in the shoulder. Reaching his hand downward, he brought it back up to his face. Seeing it was covered in blood, he started to cry like a baby.

Standing over Mickey with a gun pointed directly at his temple, the young street-trained goon couldn't do anything but laugh. "Come on, now. I know you ain't lying there crying like some little pussy, is you? Earlier today, you and your boy was some damn bosses. Y'all was making major moves; about to take over the city with that fucking fake-ass kush." He smacked Mickey upside his head with his free hand. "Matter of fact, nigga, where my bread for that damn reggie y'all sold me like I'm some green-ass bama off the farm? You need to run my shit before we kill your black ass. You don't wanna be going to hell and shit owing motherfuckers. I bet the devil don't even like shit like that, you heard? You know, on some old pride and principle shit, you feel me?" He then kicked Mickey dead in the face, busting his lip and teeth. "And I need a li'l something something extra for some new kicks. You got your blood all on these; ole, soft, bleeding, crying-ass bitch!"

Gee laughed at his little homeboy and went to the back of the crib knowing Mickey was done. Looking for Stackz with his gun still drawn, Gee found his big brother looking out the bathroom window which was wide open. Stackz was irate as the pair checked the rest of the house, going from room to room. Gee went into the far rear located bedroom. Raising his shoe, he kicked the door open with his gun ready to shoot. He saw no one in the room except for two red-nosed thoroughbred beauties in the corner that he'd startled out of their peaceful sleep. Covering his face with his shirt, Gee wondered how anyone could stand being in a room, let alone a house, that smelled like this. The floor was saturated with multitudes of old clothes that seemed to be dumped outta more than twenty or so torn green garbage bags. The puppies, of course, had made themselves at home by not only sleeping on the mildew, discarded clothes, but urinating and shitting on them as well. Seeing that the closet door was half-open, Gee kept his gun ready. As he crept up, he pulled the door open and rushed to take a few steps backward. A stench hit him instantly more horrid and overwhelming than the original funk upon entering the apparent puppy palace. Checking the closet, he discovered it to be packed with tons of more feces and puppy-pissed-on-clothing so piled high it was ridiculous.

Returning to the front of the dwelling, Stackz started to feel like their time was running out being inside the house. He knew it wasn't safe or smart to be held up, posted in a weed spot. Ordering Mickey to shut the fuck up with all that whimpering and begging, Stackz asked him if he was always such a bitch. He asked him if he was in pain. Of course, Mickey's response was yes as he foolishly asked them to call 911.

"Don't worry. You won't be in pain for long. We got somewhere to be, so we'll make it quick."

The air in the house was thick with the dread of death. It was imminent, and Mickey knew there was no way out; yet he continued to plead. The young boy went over to the makeshift table scooping up all the kush and the reggie. Gee and Stackz sat a hysterical Mickey upright. Gee mentioned to Stackz that Mickey's crying ass needs to be dealt with like you would a nagging bitch.

Stackz quickly agreed with a smile on his face. Walking throughout the crib, he looked around for what he would use to do as his brother suggested. Finally, he found what he was searching for; a nylon dog leash. Sure, the metal clamp was broken off, but the nylon itself was good and strong. Stackz tested it by wrapping each end around his hands, then pulling hard. Gee looked at his brother and gave him two thumbs-up. He and Stackz always joked about choking crybaby bitches for a good solid minute; it always worked to get them to shut up, and Mickey was starting to cry just like a bitch.

Before Mickey knew it, Stackz was standing behind him. As his eyes grew wide, the leash was wrapped tightly around his neck. Stackz pulled on the leash using all his jailhouse-chiseled body strength. "Yup, it was all good when you and your boys tried to play me like I was some duck, green-ass motherfucker! Y'all thought it was all fun and games then; so laugh now, nigga. Laugh now. Had me have to get rid of my favorite whip and a guy was straight hungry that night. Man, fuck you."

When his victim fell over toward the floor, he planted his shoe literally in the spine of Mickey's back for more leverage, causing his Adam's apple to bulge out even more. Strangling the breath out of his lungs as he kicked, snatching at the leash, Stackz tightened his grip, trying his best to snap Mickey's neck. Gee was beyond elated watching his sibling put in work. Ghoulishly, he even smiled, taunting Mickey as he reached out to him in one last attempt at mercy help. Finally, Mickey stopped resisting death and gave in to Stackz's will.

Stackz was breathing heavy. He had a look on his face the average person would swear mirrored the devil himself. He didn't take any great pleasure in killing; but business is business. And as far as he was concerned, Mickey and Rank were just that: unfinished business.

"Yeah, two down; one to go. That other motherfucker got away, but we'll catch up with him one day. He too much of a bug to stay in hiding," Stackz declared. "It's only a matter of time."

As the murderous trio looked for any clues as to where Mickey's cohort Rank might have slipped away to, they also collected a few other items. The young warrior had already taken the weed off the table, so he was good on that payback for his ruined sneakers. Gee found two more ounces of kush, a tiny plastic baggie half-filled with pills, and an old starter pistol in the dilapidated kitchen cabinet. With what they found, including the two puppies and Mickey relieved of his poor excuse of a life, the three exited the trap, on to finish the remainder of their day; no worries.

Underneath the gigantic pile of clothing Leela lay as perfectly still as she possibly could. Holding her breath from the awful stench of the garments she wanted to die. However, in reality, if she was seen moving or breathing, her wish would have been instantly granted. Leela might have been a tough tone talker when it came to Ava and her mother, and maybe with the hoes in the street, but Gee was an entirely different animal. He never tolerated her bullshit for too long before putting his foot up her ass; much like Devin used to do. But this was betrayal; it was not the same as simply running off at the mouth. Leela knew if Gee discovered her nonloyal, shady, two-faced ass hiding in this closet, it'd be lights out, for sure. She was as good as dead. She wouldn't be able to suck or fuck her way out of this situation—No matter how long they'd been banging. She wanted to call 911 but had left her cell in the room where she'd been sleeping. She was all alone. No one was coming to her aid.

The smell was close to unbearable. *Please, God, please. I'm begging you, God. Please let me live!* Leela prayed all types of lies to God. She prayed if she lived through this she would get her life together. Get her kids and move out of Detroit for good. She'd treat her mama right. Stop fucking random men for sport. *I'ma change. I'ma change starting right now. Fuck, I swear, God; right now! Please, damn!* Leela figured since it was God that woke her up off that filthy box spring instead of the sound of Rank closing the door, and God who had her go in the hallway to go get some water, enabling her to dash in the dogs' domain and take refuge underneath this mountain of mouth-vomiting animal-drenched waste, he'd step in and spare her life now as well.

Leela braced herself hearing not only Gee's, but Stackz's eager-to-kill voice as well. She wondered if Ava was with him, but knew her little sister would never tolerate or participate in anything as off the chain and vile as this. She wasn't cut like that. What was jumping off now was more her own style, but Leela wasn't trying to live that life right now, either. Terrified, she couldn't see who kicked the bedroom door in, but she heard them pause, walk over toward the closet, then leave the room. She was scared they might have fired a round or two into the pile of clothes she was in, but once again thanked God it didn't take place.

Leela's heart hurt from beating so fast. She could faintly hear Mickey from the front room moaning. She had no idea whatsoever where Rank was or what they were doing to him. Leela kept thinking, if only the houses on each side of this spot weren't vacant someone would hear Mickey's voice and possibly call the police. She prayed more lies to God as she tried blocking out the agonizing sounds of her friend moaning, begging to live.

CHAPTER TWENTY-FIVE

Leela came out of hiding. With caution, she crept slowly toward the front of the house. As she did, she prayed that the coast was clear. Having had waited twenty minutes or so before coming out—which seemed like forever—she could taste the smell of piss in her throat. As she moved closer down the hallway, she stopped in her tracks. She wanted to throw up. What she was seeing was unbelievable. Mickey's body was lying on the floor. With blood everywhere, a dog leash around his neck and his eyes wide open, Leela was stunned. Covering her mouth, she screamed into her hand as tears streamed down her face. She wanted to check to see if he was still alive, but her legs wouldn't let her move. She was shook, frozen with fear.

Moments later, she heard someone coming back into the house from the side entrance. Her eyes widened, and she began to hyperventilate. She couldn't breathe, her legs shook uncontrollably. Frightened, she stared at the door praying it wasn't Gee and Stackz coming back for her. As the footsteps got closer, time moved in slow motion in her mind. Squeezing her eyes shut, horrified of who would walk through the door, she took a deep breath, still tasting piss. Waiting to be killed, Leela heard the footsteps get closer . . . then stop. She knew whoever it was that had come in the house was now standing in the room with her. Leela still wanted to run away but strangely, couldn't move a muscle in her body.

Eyes still shut tight, she heard a familiar voice call out her name. Relieved, she opened her eyes to see Rank had come back to the house after jumping out of the bathroom window. Her body gave out as she dropped to her knees, thankful it was him and not Gee and them coming back. Rank looked over on the far side of the room and saw his manz Mickey lying on the floor dead. First, Devin, now, Mickey. Rank lost it and began punching the wall until the plaster fell out and his knuckles began to bleed. Tears fell from his eyes and anger built inside of him. This was worse than Devin being gone; he and Mickey had been day one homeboys.

Rank gathered himself together and kneeled down next to Mickey, looking at him. Out of respect, he tried closing Mickey's eyelids, but eerily, they were stuck open. Leela cried even more watching that scene play out. Rank was messed up as well. Digging into his own pocket, he pulled out a small handful of pills and tossed them into his mouth. Chewing them up, he ran over to Leela, grabbing her by the arms. Heartbroken and furious, he demanded to know every single thing about Gee and Stackz she knew. Leela never saw the look that was on Rank's face before. Needless to say, it scared her. Rank stood up, telling her they had to get outta Dodge as soon as possible. If they got caught in the house with a dead body, they'd be years tied up in jail and court trying to explain. As Leela ran in the room to gather some of her belongings, Rank went to get the stash.

"It's gone! It's fucking gone!" He knew the weed out in the open would more than likely be ghost, but not the entire bag. "What the fuck! Them grimy bitches got every damn thing. I swear they gonna die for all this bullshit!"

Rank held his head with both hands as he shook it. He thought to himself what the hell he was going to do next. With all the work gone and so little money in his pocket, he knew he was hit. Dispirited, he remorsefully went back over to Mickey's dead body. Hoping they hadn't beaten him to the punch, he went through his deceased friend's pockets. As luck would have it, he pulled out a few hundred dollars that had blood on it and shoved it in his own pocket, and then was ready to bounce.

With little loot, no place to stay, on the run, and two of his boys dead at the hands of the same man, Rank was at his wit's end. He had no choice but to kill them all before they caught up with him. Soaring high off pills, he and Leela rode around on the back streets of Detroit, hoping not to be seen. They found themselves miserable, practically living out of Rank's car while he plotted on Stackz and his people. Leela suggested to Rank that they just leave the city, and he snapped on her, announcing he was not going nowhere until Stackz and the fools that killed Mickey were dead.

Leela urged him to stop popping pills because he wasn't thinking clearly. She stood up to him, telling him he was going to mess around and get both of them killed. "It gotta end sometime."

Rank got pissed off. He informed Leela she was welcome to get the fuck on. He wasn't making her stay with him. "You got me all the way fucked up. Matter of fact, having your ass trailing behind me is getting stale anyway."

Leela didn't appreciate how Rank was speaking to her, but had to put up with it for the time being. She was afraid to go back to her mother in fear of Stackz looking for her there. And, of course, she couldn't trust Ava because she was too far gone on Stackz. Rank was her only hope. Once, maybe twice, Leela thought about going to the police, but ruled that out in fear of being locked up for an assault warrant she had pending. She was stressed out, depressed, and pregnant. It had been almost a month since Mickey's untimely death, and Rank was no closer to catching up with Stackz as the day it happened. It was like he was a dog chasing his tail. Mickey's funeral had come and gone, and neither Rank nor Leela went to pay their respect because they didn't know if they would end up in the basement cooler themselves. This life on the run was getting old to Leela, especially since she was only weeks away from showing. The mother of three knew she had to figure something out soon.

Stackz was back to business and on top of his hustle after putting Mickey to sleep for good. Things couldn't have been better in his personal life. Saying he was in love was an understatement. He was gone. However, he was not alone. Ava was still posted by her man's side and enjoyed living the high life. Stackz had convinced her to stay with him after he'd returned home from running up in Mickey and Rank's weed spot, telling her it wasn't safe for her to be at her house. Ava was not used to being a hand puppet for no man. She wasn't like her sister Leela who did exactly what she was told and would bow down if a dude was spending cash.

Ava soft grilled Stackz. Not to the point of becoming policelike, but enough for him to tell her to not ask questions she really didn't want to know the answer to. She had many things she wanted to know but opted not to press Stackz further. Ava trusted him and believed he could do no wrong. She'd fallen in love with Stackz in a short amount of time. The hardened murderer on parole had given and showed her a world any woman in her right mind could only dream of.

Since putting her sister out, the house was relatively empty anyway. There was no loud music playing all times of the day and night, no wannabe thugs pulling up in front, blowing their horns for Leela to come out, no one there sneaking up to her bedroom, stealing her clothes, and no one there asking to borrow money on the regular and never repaying it. Ava's house, just like her life, had taken a rapid and drastic change . . . all for the better. In between school and work and spending time with Stackz, she only went by her place to check on it and pick up the mail.

Ava was fully aware Leela had fallen out with their mom and was nowhere to be found as of late, but she couldn't make that her main concern. Leela had been pulling disappearing acts and stunts like this since they were in their early teens, so it was no big deal. Even Leela's three small children didn't seem to give a fuck where she was at; so life went on without her presence.

CHAPTER TWENTY-SIX

It had been nearing two solid weeks since Rank and Leela had been on the run. Quickly tapping out of cash and options, the desperate pair had to think smart if they wanted to survive. People who they once believed to be their friends had turned their backs on them. The connect refused to front Rank any more product, and the word was out in the streets that Rank had run off and left his best friend Mickey to get killed by some unknown assailants. And, of course, by not attending the funeral services, or at least blessing Mickey's people with cash assistance to help bury him, Rank seemed all the more guilty of shitting on Mickey.

Leela, of course, was fighting her own battles and demons with suspicions of guilt . . . turning her back on her sister Ava, who'd, up until the moment she'd thrown her out, had been nothing but good to her, and even more sadly, abandoned her children, not even bothering to call and check on their well-being. She knew Stackz and Gee wanted her dead just as bad as they wanted Rank dead. She wanted to go home, but couldn't. She wanted to call the police and tell them what she knew about both Devin's and Mickey's untimely demises, but dare not, knowing she'd really have a street bounty on her head then.

Almost down to point zero in revenue, Leela told Rank about an old woman that was close to her grandmother when she was alive. She informed him that she always helped people in need. Leela convinced Rank that they could go to her place for at least an afternoon and get some rest.

"She doesn't need to know all our business or nothing about us trying to stay underground. You know, just that we stopped by and wanted to get a bite to eat. I'm telling you, the old lady takes food donations for the church so she keeps food. We can get a hot meal and maybe mess around and take a shower." Leela ran her fingers through her tangled weave. "I mean, we do need to get ourselves together."

Rank looked at the gas needle, smelled his underarms, and listened to the grumbling sounds of hunger as they drove to nowhere particular. Hearing Leela's claim the elderly woman always had some roasts, fried chicken, corn, greens, and cakes and pies on deck, he asked his female partner in crime which way they should turn to get to the food. En route, Leela also told Rank that whenever she and Ava used to go to church with their grandmother, the old lady would always show up every Sunday with a lot of gold and diamonds on. She suggested when they left the old woman's house, maybe they could take the jewelry with them so they could get their empty pockets off craps.

The old woman, Mrs. Baines, lived alone on the far West Side. She had no family left in Detroit. Her son, his wife, and their children moved out of state when the city jobs started a mass layoff. With no other opportunities, he opted to relocate down South. He wanted and begged his mother to go with him. Mrs. Baines, however, wouldn't go. Not only did she feel she was too old in life to make such a big move, she believed Detroit is where she wanted to die and be buried, next to her husband.

After awhile, her son stopped asking and calling every week; now she was lucky if it was once a month. Yet, she felt as long as she had her church family, she'd be good.

Just finishing have cooked several meals for the next few days, Mrs. Baines always prepared enough to make it light on herself. After leaving the pots on the stove to cool off, she stepped out of the hot kitchen and into the living room. Not expecting anyone, she was startled to hear a knock at the door. Searching for her cane, she thought about leaving it in the corner and navigate past the coffee table, but knew that wasn't a good idea seeing how she stumbled in there a few days back.

Hearing the person knock once more, Mrs. Baines didn't want to be rude and keep whomever waiting, so she took her chances, no cane in hand. Moving slowly, she finally reached the front door. Peeking out the small window, she smiled recognizing little Leela, her old dear friend's granddaughter. Pulling her housecoat together so she wouldn't catch a draft, Mrs. Baines excitedly unlocked the door for Leela.

Missing the past and most of the people that were in it, she was elated as she let her inside. "Come on in, child. How have you been? I'm so glad to see you." The woman patted Leela on the arm. "And where are those babies of yours? Did you bring them? I showl wouldn't mind seeing them again."

"It's good to see you too, Mrs. Baines. How old are you now? You look so pretty. You don't look a day over fifty," Leela smiled as she searched the living room with her eyes; low key. "Naw, I'm sorry. The kids couldn't come this time. They're at the house with my mother."

The old woman blushed and waved her hand at Leela and said, "Child, stop lying. I'm old and tired looking. I'll be eighty-seven next week, God-willing. What brings you over today, baby? And you bring them kids next time, you hear?"

Leela thought it best to be honest; well, at least halfway honest with Mrs. Baines. So she did just that, hoping things didn't have to be done the hard way. "Well, the truth is, I'm in a little situation right now. I need a place to stay just for tonight." Leela knew if she wanted to get what she wanted, she had to pile it on thick; the same way she did when trying to finesse money from some dude. "See, I'm into it with Ava and my mom. I keep trying to get her to stop drinking so much, and she told me to mind my business, she was grown. Well, she threw me out."

"That's a shame, Leela. I thought your momma would have gave up drinking that poison after all these years."

"Me too, but she don't wanna listen to me. Ava told me I was wrong too for telling Momma she need to stop drinking. Ava said I was wrong for telling Momma what to do in her own house."

"No, child, you done told her right." Mrs. Baines easily agreed while Leela helped her sit down in a chair near the plastic-covered sofa.

Leela knew it was time to put the icing on the cake. "I thought I was right too, until they both ganged up on me and threw me out. My momma, at least, let the kids stay. I didn't have or know anywhere else to go, until I thought about you."

After taking in all of Leela's sob story, the old, often lonely, woman replied, "I guess it won't hurt any. Sure, you can spend the night."

Leela was relieved. So far, things were going as planned. Asking the elderly woman if she could please have a glass of water, the response, of course, was yes. When Mrs. Baines returned, Leela had unlocked the door allowing Rank to come inside the house. He'd been waiting outside the entire time, hoping not to be seen. Mrs. Baines wasn't happy to see a strange man standing in her living room. She was scared and didn't know what to say or think.

Before she could get a chance to react either way, Rank revealed his gun, pointing it at her. Speaking in tongues and begging the good Lord to protect her from the wicked hand of Satan, the blessed senior citizen cursed both Rank and Leela, condemning them both to hellfire.

Leela felt some sort of way. Having a flashback that her mother predicted she was on her way to hell as well, she snapped. In between living in the streets, all the death she'd been exposed to, and being pregnant, her mind was gone. In the dark zone, she began talking real nasty to the old woman, as if she was some sort of stranger out to do her harm. Not caring that her grandmother was probably turning over in her grave at the way Leela was treating her longtime friend and church member, she sucked her teeth, fed up with people's judgments.

With resentment, Leela ordered Mrs. Baines to sit down and cut all the praying and promises of God to bring down his mighty hand of wrath. Picking up a nearby Bible, Mrs. Baines refused to comply, shouting, "Praise Jesus, praise his name," even louder. An extremely hungry and mentally tired Leela had just about as much as she was willing to take. To Rank's surprise, who was still pointing the gun at the woman, Leela stormed across the room, running up in Mrs. Baines's face. Drawing back her hand, Leela brought her palm down, slapping the elderly woman's dentures clear out of her mouth. The force of the blow was so hard, poor Mrs. Baines dropped to the floor next to her teeth. As she held the side of her face crying for leniency, she asked Leela if she was smoking that crack rock that was ruining the community.

"Damn, shut the fuck up, old hag. I never like your holier-than-thou ass anyhow." Leela spewed more words of hatred directed toward the dedicated prayer warrior.

After knowing Leela all this time, Rank had never seen this side of her emerge. He knew she was basically down for whatever, seeming not to give a fuck about much of nothing, but somehow, this old woman had struck a nerve where Leela was concerned. Whatever the case was that had his female cohort on ten, showing no mercy, Rank couldn't worry about it now. He had to do his part to ensure they'd be able to eat whatever that was that had the house smelling so good and not to forget the sack of jewelry that was promised.

Surprised to find Mrs. Baines actually still had a house phone, he ripped the cord out of the wall, using it to tie her up. With her face red, on the verge of turning black, she started praying out loud once more. Not trying to keep hearing God, Jesus, the Savior, or Jehovah's name anymore, Leela swore she'd stump Mrs. Baines's mouth shut if she gummed out one more single word. With that understood, Rank and Leela proceeded to ransack the house, looking for anything of value.

Coming up with a little less than $200 and some loose change, Leela knew they were lucky to get that much out of an old person's house. Most seniors kept their money in the bank, only taking out small amounts at a time. Leela also found an old style .22 in the woman's stocking drawer and tucked it in her pocket, not letting Rank know; just for her on protection against anything in the streets, as well as him if he ever flipped out on her. Rank gathered up all the jewelry Mrs. Baines had on her person and lying on the dressers, as well as in a medium-size sparkly covered box. Leela was convinced they'd hit the mother lode. She convinced Rank to not waste another moment. He could go to the pawn shop so they could get on.

"Listen, Rank, don't pawn the stuff; just sell it outright," Leela instructed, trusting that he'd come back and not strike out on his own.

Rank located the keys to Mrs. Baines's car. He wisely took hers, leaving his own car parked deep back in the driveway. While they were alone, her grandmother's friend tried to reason with Leela. She begged her to stop this madness at once and pray to God for forgiveness. Not trying to hear anything the bruised-faced old biddy had to say, Leela paced the living room back and forth waiting for Rank to return. With nothing else to do to waste time, Leela looked over the fireplace at the multitudes of family photos of the woman's grandkids.

Suddenly overwhelmed with shame of never giving her young kids the life they deserved, Leela was close to tears. Taking her cell out of her back pocket, she decided to do something she had failed to do since leaving her mother's front porch; check on her seeds. Their fathers were not in their lives, and for the past few weeks or so, neither was she. After dialing her mother's number, she braced herself for an onset of a verbal assault. Receiving no answer, Leela told herself she'd call back later; that is, if it was still weighing heavy on her black heart.

Ninety minutes dragged by. Hearing a car pull up on the side of the house in the driveway, Leela assumed it had to be Rank finally coming back. She'd tried to reach his cell phone once or twice and didn't receive an answer. Peeking out from behind the dark red lace curtains, Leela smiled, knowing he hadn't deserted her as she thought he might. Joyfully meeting him at the front door, her enthusiasm was not returned by a twisted-faced Rank.

Bursting through the doorway, he reached his hand deep into the grocery plastic bag. Digging out a handful of the jewelry he'd stolen from the bedroom, Rank's aim was perfect, hitting Mrs. Baines in her already swollen, bruised face. Just as Leela had done earlier, Rank ran up

in the old-enough-to-be-his-mother's-mother's-mother's
face, yelling and cursing every foul word he could think
of.

"What happened? What's wrong, Rank? What's the
deal that got you so pissed? And why you bring all this
stuff back?" Leela stood over to the side letting him take
all his aggressions about whatever on Mrs. Baines. *Better
this bitch than me.*

Rank rubbed his trembling hand back across his hair,
then down across his face. "What's wrong with me?
What's wrong with my fucking black ass?" he fumed,
ready to explode. "Okay, how about they laughed me
damn near out the building at the pawn shop about this
fake-ass jewelry!"

"Fake?" Leela repeated, glancing over at Mrs. Baines.

"Yeah, fake as fuck. I mean, you had me all up there
on front street arguing these old Jew motherfuckers that
this bullshit some old priceless heirlooms. Yeah . . .
right, this shit straight garbage; all of it! Got me looking
a damn fool!"

Leela rolled her eyes, shaking her head. Walking into
the kitchen and over to the stove, she lifted the lids off
the tops of the pots of food the old woman had cooked.
Leela had the food on a low simmer, hoping to eat a good
meal to celebrate all the money Rank was going to bring
home from the pawn shop. However, she was used to
disappointments in her life and men not doing what they
said they would do; even though this cliché in the Matrix
wasn't directly on Rank.

Rank finally calmed down. He was starving and not
once protested when Leela told him it was time to eat and
to come fix himself a plate. With the nerve to sit at the
woman's dining-room table, the ruthless pair carried on
as if they really lived in Mrs. Baines's house and she was
no more than an old dishrag or towel lying on the floor
near the fireplace.

Having eaten almost everything the woman had prepared for two days, Leela opened up the freezer. Rambling through it, she took out a pack of pork chops to unthaw so she could fry them later. Rank, like Leela, had made himself at home. He had gotten comfortable on the sofa after kicking his shoes off. Finally finding a black-and-white movie on the old box-style TV, he was about ready to doze off. Just as the old woman shot her shot with Leela, she tried to talk to Rank. Not in the mood to hear her mouth, especially because he blamed her for sending him on a dummy mission to the pawn, Rank promised to her and God if she didn't shut up, he'd stuff his filthy sock in her mouth.

Leela was onto something entirely different. She went into the woman's bedroom and searched through her drawers once more. Finding a fresh clean pair of granny panties and an old religious-themed T-shirt, Leela stripped down and went to take a long, hot bath. Refreshed, but tired, she curled up in the woman's bed taking a nap.

While Rank and Leela were out committing petty crimes and home invasions on the elderly, Stackz and Ava had grown closer. Stackz had got behind Ava in her side hustle. Allowing her to make top dollar, he'd helped her step up her game up by sending people her way for phony paperwork and scripts that had major funds to spend. Business was good for Ava. Not only was she bringing in big money, Stackz was still giving her the world. Ava's money was hers to do with however she pleased.

After she had come home from the doctor's office, she and Stackz had a long talk. Stackz asked Ava if she felt she had enough money saved up to feel comfortable.

Letting her know that although he sent customers her way, he still didn't want to keep running the risk of her one day getting caught up. Getting that understood, Stackz then revealed he felt it was time for them to take things to the next level; all the way. He was ready for her to meet some of his and Gee's immediate family; not his street family, but blood. His first cousin's little girl was having a birthday party at Chuck E. Cheese in a few days. Telling her to bring Leela's kids, her nephew and nieces, Ava was elated. She was beyond happy Stackz was letting his guard down more and more with her; showing his affection was as genuine as hers.

CHAPTER TWENTY-SEVEN

Thirty-nine hours had passed since Rank and Leela had brazenly taken over Mrs. Baines's longtime home. They had cruelly put the old woman in the spare room, tying her up to the metal bed frame at night. It was late Saturday evening, and Leela was feeling charitable. With a glass of water in her hand, she'd opted to give the old lady her medication she claimed she needed.

In that moment in time, the elderly woman reminded Leela of her grandmother when she was just a small child. Strangely, it was if Mrs. Baines was reading her mind. Even though she'd been ordered by both Rank and Leela to keep her mouth shut, she began talking to her friend's granddaughter about the good ole days; the days when she and Ava were young children and how different their personalities were. How her friend always seemed to favor Leela over her spoiled younger sister. The old woman's memories were touching Leela's rotten-to-the-core spirit.

Leela knew what she was doing was way out of order. For the first time since they'd invaded Mrs. Baines's home, she felt her conscience kick in. Lowering her head in shame, Leela quickly walked out of the room, leaving the old lady still tied up with the TV on so she could watch it to keep herself company. Back in the living room, Leela found herself once more staring at the family photos of the old woman's grandkids on the mantle. Feeling some sort of way, she maternally thought of her own kids and the unborn child she was carrying by Devin. Not wanting to face the reality that she was no more than an unfit mother and a monster, Leela began laying all the various framed pictures facedown on the mantle. *Get it together, girl. I'm just emotional and fucked up in the head right now! I been down this road before! Being pregnant will do that to a bitch.*

Taking his attention away from a movie he was watching, Rank studied Leela's movements closely, sensing something was off. "You, crazy bitch, over there. Fuck is wrong with you? What you going through?"

"Nothing, nosey nigga, what's wrong with you?" Leela snapped back, ready to go on the defense over her gloomy state of mind. Wanting to have a small bit of privacy, she went into the bathroom. After turning on the water in the sink, she pulled out her cell phone. Saying a prayer that she could hold her temper down to a bare minimum, the wayward daughter dialed her mother's number again. Despite what people said about her over the years, Leela was not a total monster. She was human like the next person. If you cut her skin, she bled red blood like the next man. Leela was unable to keep holding out from at least talking to her kids and her disrespectful mom any longer. It had been weeks since she'd spoken to any of her family members, including Ava's two-faced snake ass. Leela felt her mother and kids were one thing. She was still very much mad at her sister and didn't care if they ever spoke again. To Leela, Ava was dead.

"Leela, what the fuck is wrong with you? I swear you the most selfish bitch I've ever known in my life. I can't believe I gave birth to your trifling ass. When you gonna do right by these damn kids and get your shit together? I keep telling you those streets don't care about you or nobody else, but you just won't hear me, will you?"

Leela's mother unleashed a verbal tirade into the phone, not giving her daughter a chance to even say hello.

"Well, damn, hello to you to, Momma," Leela sarcastically got a word in. "I didn't call you to hear no sermon about how you feel about me or what I'm doing wrong in my fucking life. I'm good with me. Now could you please put my oldest on the phone?"

"Naw, bitch, I can't!"

"Oh, so it's like that," Leela raged. "You not gonna let me speak to my own damn kids. That's messed up for real! Yous a real bitch for that, Momma!"

Leela's mother had just about enough of her firstborn running off at the mouth. This was the first time in weeks she had a free moment to herself and was going to celebrate with a bottle. "Look, you selfish whore. Trust me, I don't have no problem whatsoever with you being a mother to these kids. Shit, *you* had them, not me. But you soon gonna find out what happens to unfit little hoes that abandon they kids!"

"Whatever, Momma, just let me speak to my damn kids and stop playing with me," Leela demanded, not trying to hear shit else.

"Look, girl, they ain't here. And even if they was, I doubt they wanna talk to your silly ass. They gone to a birthday party at Chuck E. Cheese with Ava and that boy, what's his name she been seeing for the last few months. They just walked out the door. I swear if I didn't know any better, I'd think them was your sister's kids, as much time as she spend with them and do for them since you call yourself disappearing. When you gonna be more like your sister Ava?"

Leela heard her mother sipping something liquid and knew off rip she was drinking alcohol as always, and she was probably drunk. "And when you going to stop drinking, lady? Can you answer that before you come on me like you done lost your mind?" Leela had no respect for her elders. She was heated because her mother was going in on her; yet, she keeps a bottle of liquor glued to her mouth like it was a glass dick that she gets paid to suck. "Know what, dear Momma? I'll get my shit together when you lead by example. Until then, stop preaching at me like your shit don't stink."

Her mother laughed out loud. "Okay, girl, you can talk about me drinking all you want. But I bet I wasn't drunk in court Thursday; me or Ava. I bet that much!"

"Court? What in the fuck?" Leela paused, not knowing what her mother was talking about or why she was back bringing up Ava's name.

"Yeah, you smart-talking little thang. Like I already said, you'll see what happens to hood rat mommas that abandon their kids. You done fucked up this time for sure! Now let me go drink to that damn fact! Bye, bitch!"

The infuriated daughter pressed the button ending the call. Picking up a bottle of lotion that was sitting on the sink, Leela smashed it against the bathroom mirror. Watching the shattered, sharp, shiny pieces fall to the ceramic floor, Leela was past a hundred and counting, thinking about all the things her mother had said and claimed. Not only had she not spoken to her kids, she'd found out her sister had them out, showboating, having a good time with the man who murdered her soon-to-be born child's father.

Who does Ava think she is? Those are my kids, not hers. Did her fake ass ask me could she take my kids anywhere? Hell naw. I don't want mines around that nigga Stackz either. Fucking asshole. If it wasn't for him wanting to prove a point and kill Devin, shit would still be good. Man, fuck him and Ava. Them bitches wanna act like it's fuck me; all right then. It's on for real! And my mother, that bitch gonna get hers too! On everything, she gonna pay!

Her touched-by-an-angel remorseful spirit Mrs. Baines
had invoked was gone. Just like that, Leela was back to
herself after speaking to her mother; vindictive, hateful,
and spiteful. Bolting out of the bathroom, she ran down
the hallway and straight up to Rank, interrupting his
time in front of the television. "Yo, it's now or never!
Nigga, you tired of running, and I am too. So peep game,
I know where this nigga Stackz is at right damn now!"

Leela put Rank up on game, informing him that her
mother had dry snitched on Stackz and didn't even
know it. In the middle of all her insults, berating Leela,
the fact that she revealed Ava and Devin's murderer
were at Chuck E. Cheese was as good as signing Stackz's
death warrant. Quick thinking, Leela told Rank that her
no-good fake sister and that ho-ass buster were either at
the location on the far West Side or the deep East Side,
seeing as there were only two in the city. "Look, all we
have to do is take the old woman's car and hit both of
them real quick. They at one or the other, and I know
his truck when I see it." Leela was in full snake mode,
counting on Rank to be rolling off E-pills and not being
able to control himself catching Stackz off guard at the
right time and right place.

Rank rubbed his chin in deep thought. After having
flashbacks of the night Devin was killed, he closed his
eyes and saw Mickey lying on the floor with his eyes
wide open and his tongue hanging out of his mouth to
one side. He remembered the pain and seemingly fresh
wounds of his own caused by the hands of one man:
Stackz. And now, thanks to Leela's drunken, loose-
lipped mother, he knew where he could find him to get
his revenge. Rank nodded his head, agreeing with her.
"Yeah, you right; it's now or never."

And just like that, once again, Leela had pulled Rank's strings to do her bidding. She knew it would be dangerous to go with Rank on his sure-to-be-murderous melee, but she said fuck it. Why not ride shotgun and get a ringside seat? After putting the play into motion, she wanted to see the look on Stackz's face when he got what was coming to him. And better than that, to bear witness to Ava's little sad, cracked face when the new man in her life, that meant more than their sister bloodline bond, was lying dead facedown in a pool of his own blood.

Swallowing a few of Rank's "get a nigga right" pills, Leela was hyped, still thinking about the hate her mother was putting in her ear. She was so bent and in the zone that she didn't care if her sister or her kids were smack-dab in the middle of the tragic situation. They could get longtime therapy later for what was about to pop off. *Fuck 'em all!* Leela's heart, or what was left of it, had gone completely cold as ice.

Trying to decide what to do with the old woman until they came back from their mission, they tossed ideas back and forth as they went to the spare room. Leela went in first, and Rank followed closely behind.

"Hey, Mrs. Baines," Leela called out to the old lady who didn't respond to hearing her name. Going over to the bed, she harshly shook her shoulder. The woman's body was flimsy, and she didn't move an inch. "Hey, wake up, old lady; don't play fucking sleep. We don't have time for no games. Not now. We got shit to do, places to be." Leela shoved the elderly woman yet again, this time harder and in the spine of her back. Mrs. Baines still had no response.

Rank moved closer toward the bed to investigate the situation. Taking the woman's wrist in his hand, he checked to see if she had a pulse. Rank felt nothing.

Letting her wrist go, it flopped down lifelessly back onto the bed. Leela and Rank simultaneously looked at each other with an *oh . . . shit* face. Already in too deep by home invading the old woman's house, now the treacherous pair could add kidnapping and premeditated murder to their résumés. At least, that's how the police, judge, and jury will react if and when it was ever discovered that Leela and Rank had been in her house uninvited.

Neither of the two had any real remorse for clearly causing the old woman's early retirement from life. In a fast-paced attempt to try to cover their tracks, they decided to straighten up the place the best they could. Hopefully, if they untied Mrs. Baines and staged her body just so, they could have it appear that she was old and just died in her sleep.

Leela and Rank hurried so they could hit the streets and tend to the business of ruining Stackz and Ava's good time.

CHAPTER TWENTY-EIGHT

Stackz and Ava picked up Leela's three kids and were headed to the birthday party for Stackz and Gee's first cousin's daughter. Ava had bought all the kids brand-new outfits to wear and got the girls' hair braided and her nephew's haircut. She made sure the kids would represent the Westbrook clan's name to the utmost.

When they got to Chuck E. Cheese, Ava reminded them to please be on their best behavior. Stackz watched his girl interact with the kids and thought to himself, *Yeah, I'll put a seed up in her ass. I see she knows how to handle the little shorties.* They entered the building, and Stackz looked around for his family. Once he located them, they turned the kids loose to join the other children who were playing with the birthday girl.

Stackz introduced Ava as his wifey to his family. The women praised him for finding a beautiful lady that looked like and carried herself like she had good sense, not the other tramps they'd seen him with from time to time. The adults were having their own party, drinking liquor they'd put in pop bottles, and going outside occasionally to smoke some weed.

Ava was happy his family accepted her and made her feel comfortable. Stackz noticed Gee, his small son, and the boy's moms coming in the building. He went and greeted them and hugged his nephew's mother like they were best buddies. Introducing her to Ava, she felt awkwardly put on the spot because, A, she didn't even know Gee had any kids, and B, Ava knew Gee had spent countless times over at her house laid up with Leela like it wasn't shit.

It was almost time to cut the cake and the birthday girl's father still hadn't arrived yet. Stackz asked his cousin where Pissy was at.

"That asshole just called saying he got held up on some business and he was on this way with my baby's new bike she's been asking for. He better have it because you know that fool is full of shit and games!"

It was nearing two hours later. The happy birthday song had been sung, the cake had been cut, and the adults had about enough of the kids. They started gathering them up to leave, but there was still no sign of Pissy. The little girl asked her mother if her daddy was here yet with her big surprise, and she disappointedly had to tell her no.

Family fun time had come to an end for the street loyal brothers. Stackz and Gee had some business on the floor that couldn't wait. Gathering both their girls and the kids, they said their farewells and headed toward the door. Seemingly in a deep conversation, Gee and Stackz walked side by side discussing how they were going to handle this and that. Gee's baby moms, Ava, and the kids followed a few feet behind the men so they wouldn't be in their mix.

Stackz was still talking to Gee as they went out the door. Distracted by what was out in front of the building, Stackz stopped dead in his tracks. Blocking the doorway crosswalk was an obviously freshly custom-painted burnt-orange Jeep Commander. As he stood speechless alongside of Gee, Stackz knew he had to be seeing things. He knew he had to be wrong. His mind *had* to be playing tricks on him.

Slowly walking around the truck, he saw the same small dent on the rear quarter panel as his Jeep and the same nick on the passenger-door handle. Stackz knew for certain when he saw the guts were the same color, this was his motherfucking truck, and this slimeball Pissy had done the unthinkable. He'd done the complete opposite of what Stackz had told him to do. Stackz warned Pissy not to be up to his shiesty ways he'd do to others and slick tag his truck instead of having it melted down as told.

Pissy hadn't seen Stackz because he was preoccupied pulling the small-size bike out of the rear of the Jeep. When he finally looked up, it was like he'd seen a ghost. "Oh, hey, Stackz," he stumbled on his words. "I didn't know you was coming to a kid's party. I mean, I ain't know you had any kids." Pissy didn't know what to say. Spending an afternoon at Chuck E. Cheese didn't seem like it would be in Stackz's DNA seeing how he had no kids, so Pissy thought the coast would be clear, so to speak. He would drive the truck just for today and have it shipped out West where he had a guaranteed sale. Now, here, he was busted; caught red-handed having had done dirt.

Stackz was infuriated that Pissy had crossed him after being warned. Heading straight for Pissy, the vein in the side of Stackz's neck bulged and started to jump. "Nigga, did you just meet me or something? What did I tell your dirty ass to do?"

"Cuz, fam, hold on. This ain't what it look like."

"Naw, nigga, it's *just* what it looks like!" Stackz ripped the bike out of birthday girl's snake-ass father's grasp. Seeing red for having been not only betrayed, but disobeyed, he threw the bike as hard as he possibly could up against the brick wall of Chuck E. Cheese.

Gee had the women go get in the vehicles and take the kids with them that had started to cry. Gee's son's mother was used to this type of drama popping off at the end of most of their family functions and get-togethers;

however, Ava was shocked to see Stackz transform back to the beast he was the day she first laid eyes on him at the restaurant. Without saying a word, she did as she was told, taking her nieces and nephew to Stackz's truck.

"Look, ho-ass nigga, ain't nothing to talk about. You done fucked up the church's money, cuz. Now run those keys before I send you on your way right here and now." Stackz had Pissy collared up against the building, shaking him up until the truck keys dropped from his hand.

Stackz signaled for Gee to come get the keys and help him get rid of the truck before he murked Pissy right on the spot for going against the grain.

"Bet. I'll have my baby momma drive my shit, and I'll drive this. Don't worry, bro, I got you," Gee replied, stepping over the frame-bent small bike, not believing the nerve of Pissy.

"Family or not, you can't cross the king and expect to keep breathing," Stackz raged with malice in his tone, letting Pissy go. Knowing he needed to calm down before he caught another body, Stackz walked away.

CHAPTER TWENTY-NINE

Stackz was on ten, furious when he got into the truck with Ava and the kids. "I told him don't fuck me. I warned that son of a bitch not to play with me," he shouted, looking at Ava dead in the face before putting the key in the ignition.

The kids had recovered from the shock of seeing the little girl's bike thrown up against the wall and were horse playing in the backseat. But all that ceased immediately seeing Stackz getting in the truck. They'd seen their mother and grandmother have enough arguments and near physical fights to know when to become invisible. The kids said nothing as their aunt looked at them with warning eyes to settle down and be on their best behavior; they did just that fearing Stackz.

"He thinks this a fucking game? Is Hasbro stamped on my forehead, or something like I'm somebody to play with?" Stackz's rage intensified as Ava remained silent.

Stackz maneuvered his way out of the Chuck E. Cheese's parking lot into traffic. He had no patience with other drivers as he darted haphazardly from lane to lane. He knew something was fishy when he hadn't heard from Pissy about the ticket for the meltdown and disappearance, but trusted him because of their longtime affiliation and family ties; obviously a big mistake. He wanted to get Ava and the kids back to her momma's house as quickly as possible so he could figure out his next move.

Ava wanted to say something to soothe Stackz's temper, but thought it was best to keep quiet in fear of him recalling the circumstances of how they first crossed paths and the underlining reason his Jeep Commander ultimately had to be ghost in the first place.

Knowing he now had to make preparations to get rid of that possibly hot truck himself, Stackz's mind-set was preoccupied. Totally off his square, he was forgetting one of the main rules of being about that life. Stackz wasn't paying attention to his surroundings. If he had been, he'd seen the black Mercury Grand Marquis following them. On a mission, Rank sat in the passenger seat shotgun as Leela drove.

Leela and Rank had shown up just in time to see their intended target getting rough with some man, then storm off to his ride, seemingly in a rage. Leela thought she saw Ava and her children inside of Stackz's truck with tinted windows when they whizzed by, but was not sure. She hated Ava's new man with all she had, blaming him for taking Devin away prematurely. She knew Devin had it coming that night, and he definitely wasn't the only man she was messing with, but her soon-to-be baby daddy was the only one willing to take her out in public, proudly showing her off. And for that, she missed him.

Making sure she kept up with the clean Range Rover, Leela grew more agitated that her children had been hanging out with her sister and Stackz, probably not once wondering where their own mother had been and if she was okay. Just as she hated Stackz, she despised Ava even more for ruining her life in general and causing their mother to turn on her. Gone off a handful of pills she'd chewed up to get in her system more quickly, she swerved, trying to keep up with Stackz. Now three cars behind, she asked Rank if he was ready to make his move and take Stackz out of the game once and for all.

"Fuck all that, you been in my stash, ho," Rank snapped at Leela, worried about his rapid decline in pills.

"So what if I have? I needed something to even me out. A bitch got shit on her mind too," Leela snarled, switching lanes when Stackz did.

Rank shook his head, not having time to argue with Leela's good thieving, trifling, pregnant ass. He was focused on Stackz's truck as he peered over the dashboard from his slumped down position. "Okay, dig . . . At this next light, be ready to pull up on the side of his ass," Rank order Leela.

Stackz, Ava, and the kids blindly had no idea what chaos was about to take place in a matter of seconds. While Stackz was still going about Pissy, Leela got closer. Rank was ducked down in the passenger seat geeked up like always off E-pills. Glancing over, he noticed Leela grinding her teeth and her arms trembling. She was gone in her head due to the pills she had taken from Rank's stash, and it showed. Nothing or no one mattered to Leela right about now but getting revenge on Stackz and her low-down, dirty, backstabbing sister.

"Make sure you kill that nigga. He don't deserve to live. He took our people outta the game, so he need to go too. Remember Devin and Mickey. Do it for them, Rank; kill that nigga." Leela hyped him up to commit murder as the next light grew closer in their sights.

Stackz had called T. L. and was barking into his phone as he came to a complete stop at the red light. Still preoccupied, the normally cautious Stackz was off his square mad at the stunt Pissy had pulled. In his own world, he paid no mind to the black car abruptly swerving over alongside him in the turning lane. Ava, still being silent, felt something bad come over her all of a sudden. Turning her head to look in Stackz's direction, she suddenly let out a bloodcurdling scream as the light turned green. Ava couldn't believe her eyes as she looked out of the vehicle. Rank was hanging out of the passenger-side window of a car pointing a gun up toward the truck and Stackz, while Leela was at the wheel.

Not one, or two, or three, or even four gunshots rang out, but seven in total as Stackz's foot simultaneously lifted off the brake. Bullet-shattered glass flew everywhere as Ava instinctively grabbed the steering wheel swiftly, veering the truck away from the car Rank was riding in. Stackz dropped his phone in his lap while yelling at Ava and the kids to get down and hurry. As low as possible in hopes of being out of harm's way, Stackz hit the gas while trying to reach for his gun that was underneath his seat to return fire.

Not being able to follow Ava's instructions on being quiet any longer, the three under-the-age-of-seven children were hysterically crying in the backseat. Ava somehow had managed to commandeer the SUV to the right, narrowly missing ramming into an oncoming car that now had the right of way. It had become total anarchy within a split second inside the Range Rover for Stackz, Ava, and the children. Stackz's truck jumped the curb and ended up coming to a stop a few inches away from a bus stop bench.

Rank had emptied the clip of his gun but was so amped up on pills he kept squeezing the trigger. Leela kept one hand on the wheel, using the other to snatch Rank by his shirt, pulling him back inside of the car. Smashing her foot onto the gas pedal, she floored it into traffic at a high rate of speed, turning left and disappearing into the far distance.

***

Stackz and Ava jumped down out of the truck. As remnants of glass fell to the pavement on Stackz's side, he felt a small trickle of blood drip down over his eyebrow. Not taking any more chances, he held his gun at his side on high alert just in case whoever was ballsy enough to pull such a stunt had any intentions on doubling back. Not immediately worried about himself, he opened the rear door on one side while Ava opened the other. With their hearts racing with fear for the little ones, they began searching the hysterically crying children for any signs of trauma. Other than a few minor cuts from flying glass, some that had struck Stackz in the face as well, all seemed to be good. Visibly shaken, tears streamed down Ava's face as she leaned against the truck to catch her breath. Stackz made his way around to the passenger side. The same exact way he'd checked the children, he checked Ava. Holding her in his arms, he asked if she'd been hit. Thankfully the answer was no.

"I saw him right before he started shooting. All I could do was scream," Ava broke all the way down, sobbing into Stackz's chest.

"Who did you see, Ava, who?" he quizzed, pulling her away from his body, looking into her face for the answer.

As the children look on terrified, their aunt was completely losing it. Ava's body was shaking. Her lips began to tremble. She started to feel dizzy. It was as if the night air was strangling her. Her throat grew dry, and she couldn't swallow, let alone speak.

Stackz was not new to people being in shock. In his line of work, occurrences like this, and sometimes fatally worse ones, popped off all the time. Placing both hands on her shoulders, Stackz shook Ava until she snapped out of what she was going through. "Ava! Ava! Listen to me, who did you see? Tell me! Who the fuck was it? Who?"

Struggling to get her mouth to form the god-awful words, she finally pushed them out. "Rank! It was Rank shooting, and Leela was driving, Stackz. My own sister was driving! She needs to be dead for what she just did. How could she, how?"

Stackz didn't say a word. At first he stood there not believing what she'd just said about her sister. As the reality of it set in good, he was infuriated all over again. Rank was one thing. He expected for him to make his play and seriously had to tip his hat for trying to go so hard with it just then. But Leela? Ava's own sister, driving a nigga around to shoot up a car with her kids in the backseat, like . . . So the fuck what? Like Ava, Stackz's emotions grew numb for any chance of allowing Leela to live. He'd seen a lot of grimy things jump off in the streets from crackheads, junkies, drunks, crooks, and criminals doing just about anything, but Stackz had never seen a woman that would sink so low as what Leela had just participated in.

"Come on, we gotta get out of here." Stackz helped Ava get back in the SUV as people began to gather around and ask questions. He thanked God the truck was still drivable as they pulled off. As he drove, Ava turned around, promising the still whimpering kids that everything was going to be okay and not to cry. But deep down inside, she knew that wouldn't be the case.

CHAPTER THIRTY

Stackz and Ava drove in silence. No longer mad about Pissy's betrayal, he couldn't believe the nerve of Leela. Whenever he caught up with Rank, he prayed Leela was there too so he could make her pay for all her sins. For every tear Ava and her three babies riding in the back of his truck shed, he'd make her suffer tenfold.

Arriving at her mother's house to drop off the traumatized kids, he first drove around the block, making sure the brazen duo were not somewhere close plotting, once more, in hopes of ambushing them. Before getting out of the truck, Ava searched through her purse, finally finding the spare key. Looking up at the house, she took notice there were no lights on in the single-family dwelling. Assuming that her mother was still over at her friend's house having some drinks and playing cards, Ava had Stackz sit in the truck with the kids while she ran in and made sure what she believed to be true was.

Still very much shaken and on edge that her own flesh and blood could be so cold and callous, Ava nervously ran to the porch of her mother's house. Peeking over the railing, she looked on the side of the house, not knowing if Leela was maybe there waiting in the shadows to try to kill her yet again. Putting her key in the front door, Ava unlocked it, then went inside the dark house. Calling out to her mom, she went from room to room, turning on lights as she went along. Ava knew her mother had a bad habit of overdoing it at times and wanted to make sure she hadn't enjoyed her break from watching Leela's three babies so much so that she was passed out cold somewhere on the floor.

After Ava's minisearch was complete, she left the living room and kitchen light on so her mother wouldn't come home to a dark house. Locking the door, Ava darted back to the truck. "I'm sorry, bae. She's not home yet, and we can't leave them here by themselves," she explained to Stackz.

"I know. Now listen, we're going to your crib real quick. I want you to get whatever else you might need for a few weeks because you're not going home until this bullshit is taken care of with Rank and ole girl." Stackz referred to Leela as ole girl, so the kids didn't know he was talking about their soon-to-be-dead mammy. "After you go grab your things, we'll just double back. Your mother will probably be home by then. Then I'ma drop you at the crib 'cause me, Gee, and T. L. gotta link up."

Ava knew what that meant and prayed to God they caught up with not only Rank but Leela as well.

Fifteen minutes after leaving Ava's mother's house, they pulled up at her place.

"Make it quick, baby," Stackz said to Ava as she got out and ran to her front door.

When Ava got upstairs and turned on the lights, she noticed right away somebody had been in there. She was instantly pissed. Her first mind told her to go back outside and get Stackz, but she bravely ventured on, praying whoever had been there was long gone now. When Ava got to her bedroom, the first thing she looked for was her jewelry box, which was gone. As her body tensed up in anger, she looked around, quickly realizing nothing else had been touched or was missing with the exception of her work bag that had a few extra blank scripts in it and her framed achievement certificates scattered on the floor with the glass smashed. Then and there, she knew Leela was the culprit. It was the only probable assumption. A real burglar would've cleaned the place totally out. They would've taken the flat-screen TVs and everything else that wasn't screwed or bolted down, not taking the time to get as personal as to care about pissing on her accomplishments.

Ava went downstairs and saw the window over the sink had been jimmied open from the outside. The only other person besides herself that knows how to get in that way is Leela. Whenever she'd be locked out, she'd roll the Dumpster to the side of the house, stand on top of it, and lift the window up. After Ava put two and two together, she hurried and gathered all her valuables that she didn't want to leave behind, just in case her crazed sister had the audacity to return. Making sure she double locked the window to at least make it a challenge for Leela if she did come back, Ava left the house.

After putting her things in the rear of the Range Rover, she hopped back in the front seat. "That ho broke in my house. She took my damn jewelry, my work bag that had a few extra scripts in it, and did some other petty bullshit." Ava was disgusted with her so-called blood's antics. "Me and that bitch are the only ones that know how to get in like she did. Trust me, it was that rotten womb-ass ho. Leela is a snake bitch. She didn't even care her kids were in here when that nigga shot at us."

Ava broke down crying once more. Stackz reassured her all would be taken care of as soon as they dropped the kids back off at her mother's house. Ava wiped her tears away, finding some comfort in his words. Putting her seat belt back on, she looked in the rear at Leela's sleeping kids, glad they didn't hear the harsh words she'd spoken about their mother.

CHAPTER THIRTY-ONE

It was as if something menacing was circulating through-out the night air as Ava and her man returned to her mother's house to drop off the children. It'd been one of those days that started off like any other; things were good, no big problems, no major issues. They'd enjoyed the day with Leela's kids, who were thankful to be out of the house, and Stackz's family, who seemed to accept her into their close-knit fold. All was well. Then *bam!* Out of the clear blue sky, things transformed within the blink of an eye. From the very moment they stepped foot outside of Chuck E. Cheese and Stackz laid eyes on that man and what she heard him say was his truck—or used to be his truck—the drama unfolded quickly and seemed to be never-ending. It was as if the devil had turned on the light switch in the middle of their calm, dimly lit serenity.

Ava had a sick sense watching Stackz transform into the shoulder to shoulder tattoo he'd proudly worn across his back for years: 100% GANGSTER. Somehow, Ava knew standing over to the side with Gee's woman and the children, the ride home and the rest of the evening would be on definite edge. And from the near-fatal and crime-filled chain of events thus far, she'd hit her mark. The sugar-to-shit evening could've, however, been much worse. They could have all been dead from the bevy of bullets Rank sent torpedoing their way, and Ava's house could've been burglarized by real thieves. As she settled back in the passenger seat, she knew there was one common factor in both of these mind-numbing actions: Leela. Her sister, her blood, her supposed-to-be best friend since birth. Ava could only pray for the girl to turn herself in to the law before not only Stackz got his hands on her, but she as well.

As Stackz tried his best to avoid the multitudes of potholes in the road, Ava couldn't imagine how the night could get any worse. He had the radio on low as to not wake up or disturb the children asleep in the rear of the truck. Stackz knew they had suffered enough trauma for the evening. In between running themselves ragged at Chuck E. Cheese, and then their own mother attempting to have them shot in what Stackz felt was a botched hood assassination, he just wanted to safely deliver them back to their grandmother the way he'd gotten them . . . alive and unharmed; well, at least, physically.

Having had ridden with his gun on his lap, Stackz parked in front of the house and checked his surroundings. He'd been caught slipping earlier and knew that could never take place again; not tonight—not ever.

Seeing the light she'd left on in the living room was now off, Ava was relieved knowing her mother had made it back home. Wanting nothing more than to take a long, hot bath at Stackz's condo, she was happy to drop her nieces and nephew off and do just that. Still cautious, she opened the passenger door, placing one foot down on the truck's running board. "Bae, hold tight real quick. I see the light I left on is off so I know my mother is back. I just wanna make sure she's not in there drunk and tripping. You know what I mean." Ava looked over at Stackz, hoping after all that had taken place this evening he was sympathetic to her dilemma. "When she gets to drinking that cheap wine, she can't function properly."

Looking up into the rearview mirror, Stackz saw the kids were still fast asleep, probably having nightmares of being cursed with such a bitter, vindictive bitch as a mother. "Ava, go ahead and see what's good with your old girl. I'm posted. And if it ain't right up in there, don't worry. Push come to shove, the little shorties can crash at my crib tonight with us. It's all good."

"Ma, we back with the kids," Ava shouted as she stood in the front doorway waiting for her mother to respond. Still in her feelings, not knowing where Leela was at or what she was capable of, Ava was spooked in the house she'd grown up in, as if she was a total stranger. Hearing nothing, she called out to her mother once more while walking into the living room turning on the lamp. "Ma, where you at? We back from Chuck E. Cheese." Ava paused, looking toward the now once again dark kitchen. Hitting the light switch, she took notice of a brown paper bag on the countertop containing a fifth of whiskey in it, verifying her mother had indeed made it home.

Closing an open drawer, Ava then double-checked that the basement door was locked as she always did when stopping by. Seeing it was, she was relieved her mother hadn't at least accidently fallen down the stairs like she had in the past when she'd been out drinking with her friends. "Ma, where you at? Them kids need to go to bed. It's getting late! Where you at?"

Nearly exhausted herself, Ava was just ready to get this terrible night over once and for all. Coming out of the kitchen, she hoped her mother was not too intoxicated and was able to take care of what should have been Leela's responsibility and burden to bear.

Standing in the hallway, Ava quickly noticed the rear bathroom light was on and headed in that direction, praying for the best, but anticipating the worst. *Damn, don't let her silly ass be passed out in that motherfucker, please.*

"Ma, Ma, are you in the bathroom or what? I know you hear me calling you. Are you in here?" Ava reached the semiclosed door. "Ma," she loudly called again, slowly pushing the door open, "are you in here?" *Oh my God, no! What in the hell?* Stumbling backward away from the bathroom, Ava couldn't believe what her eyes were seeing. She wanted to scream out to Stackz for help. Unfortunately, her mouth couldn't seem to form the words. The night had just officially gone straight to hell.

CHAPTER THIRTY-TWO

"Yeah, I think I ripped a hole through the side of that motherfucker's head! Did you hear your ho-ass sister screaming and shit? Dumb bitch. Yeah, I think I hit 'em both. Yo, Leela, did you see that shit? That shit was live!" Rank was going on and on about what he'd just done. Still gone off the pills he was on, he felt like he could take on the world and win.

Equally as high as Rank, Leela's adrenalin was soaring for an altogether different reason. For her, it was more personal. Although deep down inside, she prayed her babies weren't shot or worse than that, dead, Leela was living her life under a brand-new set of rules she was making up as she went along. She was fed up with being a mother and having to deal with all the responsibility that came with it. She'd made up her mind back at Mrs. Baines's house she was going to get rid of Devin's kid even if she had to throw herself down a flight of stairs to do it. *Fuck one more mouth to feed.* Leela kept her eyes focused on the road as her thoughts raced.

If the devil was on her side, hopefully, Ava had taken one of those rounds intended for Stackz. She'd be done with Ava outdoing her all the time and people going around looking down on her because she wasn't as smart as Ava, as pretty as Ava, and as wise as Ava to not have three different deadbeat baby daddies. Leela felt like now that Ava was dead, it could finally be—fuck Ava! People would say why wasn't Ava as smart, pretty, and wise as Leela to avoid taking a bullet to the head and staying alive. Now would be Leela's time to shine.

Jointly, they decided it'd be in their best interest to get a new vehicle. Wanting to avoid contact with any of Stackz's people and the law that may have recognized the car they were in, Leela pulled over so they could devise a quick plan of their next move. Knowing they would need some extra cash, she suggested that they creep by her sister's house because she knew she had a few items of value they could flip right away. Pulling up a block over from Ava's house, Rank slid over to the driver's seat after Leela had gotten out. Paranoid off the pill high she was still on, Leela darted down the debris-filled alley and cut across a few vacant lots. In no time flat, she was rolling one of the black garbage cans underneath the kitchen window and breaking into the place she'd last called home.

Once inside, she went down in the basement, then up the stairs leading to Ava's part of the house. Running down the hallway, Leela knew just what she was looking for. Flicking on the bedroom light, she snatched her sister's jewelry box off the top of the dresser, grabbed her work bag off the chair, then maliciously raised her hand, knocking a couple of Ava's awards to the floor, stamping on them a few good times before she left.

By the time Leela had made it back to the car, Rank had already set up a buy with his used-to-be connect so he could cop some more pills. The only thing he needed and was counting on was Leela coming back with either some bread or something else she claimed Ava had they could quickly turn into cash.

"Okay, cool, you hit a lick. Just give me the jewelry and I'll go get us a new stash, dump this car, and get one we can pimp a few more days," Rank plotted, still living in the celebration from believing he'd killed Stackz.

Not wanting to part with the jewelry, she'd been trusting Rank all of this time and he'd never crossed her once. So against her hood-raised judgment, she agreed. "All right then, just take me by my mother's house. Just like it's fuck Stackz and Ava, well, it's fuck her too!"

Rank had watched Leela turn into a complete savage since they'd teamed up on the run. He thought she might've at least been in her emotions about her kids and Ava being in that truck when he let loose, but she seemed more eager than he was to start shooting.

CHAPTER THIRTY-THREE

Ava's eyes widened, darting from the blood on the sink, to the blood on the side of the tub, to the bloody handprint that was smeared down the wall. Stumbling backward, she quickly got herself together. She had no choice. There her mother was, sprawled out on the black and pink ceramic tiled floor, facedown in a small pool of blood.

Running into the bathroom, Ava bent down to see if her mother was at least still breathing. With care, she placed one hand on the side of her mother's face, positioning the other on her waist. Turning her over, Ava could easily smell she reeked of wine and liquor and had urinated on herself. Ava was hurt seeing her mother in this condition. Her mouth was busted and the side of her jaw bruised as she fought to speak. Ava assumed she'd lost her balance trying to make it to the bathroom and fell like so many other times in the past. Ava felt disgusted having been down this road with her alcoholic mother on more than several occasions throughout the years. The entire night had been an utter nightmare . . . now this. Ava shook her head.

"Damn, Ma, you must've hit your face and mouth on the sink when you fell. You need to stop all this madness!" Growing queasy at the strong pungent smell taking over the bathroom, Ava carefully stepped over her mother's drunken body. With intentions of getting some air, she moved the shower curtain over to one side. Reaching her arm up to unlock the window, Ava was suddenly knocked into the glass. Feeling a hard object then strike the rear of her head, Ava's hand grabbed ahold of the curtains, snatching them off the rod as she fell to her knees. Dazed and confused as to what had happened, she could barely think, let alone stand up. What had to be her own blood poured down on her neck, then started to drench her shirt.

After a few brief seconds of being on her knees, Ava felt the intense onset of the worst pain she'd ever felt in her life. She didn't have time to get herself together or gather her thoughts as she heard Leela's voice calling her every name she could think of. Before Ava could say anything, her older sister snatched her up by the back of her collar, dragging her across their mother's body and out into the hallway.

"So you and that asshole parked out front still alive, huh?" Leela bowled Ava's unsteady body into the wall before kicking her in the side two good times. With the hammer she'd use to bust her sister's head wide open down at her side, Leela grew more enraged as well as deranged. "Damn, I guess Rank's aim ain't as good as his dumb ass think. But, hey, it ain't no thang. I'll take care of you, then Stackz myself, so fuck it."

Ava reached one hand up to the rear of her head while keeping the other wrapped around her stomach and waist. Seeing that Ava called protecting herself from any more of her attacks, Leela struck again, this time bringing the sole of her shoe brutally down on Ava's face. Ava let out a grunt, followed by a few moans and groans. Finally catching her breath, she spoke out.

"Leela, why in the fuck you doing this to me, Momma, and the kids? What's wrong with you? Why? Have you lost your damn mind?"

"Fuck Momma." Leela glanced back in the bathroom where their mother was still lying, bleeding from the mouth. "Her motherfucking ass talk too damn much. That's why I made a special trip to come over here and tap that ass. Then the bitch gonna show me some papers from the court saying you and her got joint guardianship over my kids. Hell naw! Fuck that sneaky bitch trying to come for my food stamps, and you too!"

"Really, Leela? You gonna do us all like that? For real?"

This wasn't the time or place for Leela to continue to answer who, what, or why with Ava. Playtime was over. "Look, I'm out here doing me, bitch, and that's fucking that." She tried kicking Ava once more but was caught off guard as her leg was grabbed and she was yanked down off her feet. Having had the hammer fly out of her hand, she and Ava were now even. Side by side on the hallway floor next to Ava, the two sisters went at it, holding nothing back. As they clashed, each giving as good as they got, the younger sibling was at a slight disadvantage considering the hammer blow to the head she'd suffered. Leela, of course, capitalized on that fact, delivering punch after punch to the open leaking wound.

Somehow, during the course of the impromptu battle, the sisters got onto their feet, but were still throwing punches. Catching Ava right underneath her rib cage with her fist, Leela used her body weight bum-rushing her up against the wall, causing a picture of both of them and their mother to eerily fall off the nail and land on the floor. Leela paid no attention to the possible omen as she kept choking the life out of Ava.

Wondering what was taking Ava so long to come back out and get the kids, Stackz decided to go in. Making sure they were still asleep, he put one up top before getting out of the truck, pistol in hand. Closing the door as quietly as possible, he crept up on the front porch. Noticing that the door was cracked, Stackz eased it open, unsure of what was really taking place on the other side. Wisely not calling out Ava's name, he slow stepped his way into the living room. Hearing what he thought was the unique sound of someone grunting, then something crashing to the floor, Stackz wasted no more time in investigation mode, smelling imminent death in the air.

Bolting down the hallway, he ran up on Leela boldly attempting to send Ava on her way. Tucking his gun in the small of his back, Stackz used both hands whiplash yanking Leela by the weave, slinging her to the ground. Reaching downward, he wrapped his hands around her throat, lifting her up to eye level. "Now, bitch, how it feel to have somebody choke your no-good ass out, huh? This shit feel good? Do it," he hissed with sheer malice in his voice. After a few more seconds of making her eyes damn near pop out of her head, he flung Leela's almost lifeless body to the floor once more. As he stood across the room trying to figure out the easiest way to kill her and be rid of the headache she'd become once and for all, Leela played the final card in her hand.

"You and that bitch Ava got me all fucked up." She'd somehow managed to reach in her pocket and pull out the janky .22 she'd stolen from old Mrs. Baines. Pointing it directly at Stackz, she halfway grinned, seeing as he couldn't reach in his back waistband to get his gun without her firing off a shot or two. "Yeah, Stackz, it ain't never ever no fun when the rabbit got the gun, is it?"

Not fearing death, Stackz took one step toward Leela, daring her to pull the trigger. Out of options, she did just that, putting three slugs into his chest area. Not made of steel, the street warrior fell to the ground. Ava, who had

I Can Touch the Bottom

recovered from being nearly strangled to death, was now hysterical as she crawled over to Stackz. Using her body to shield his from taking any more bullets, Ava sobbed, begging Leela to show them both some mercy.

Leela was now on her feet feeling victorious. As she boasted and bragged about all the things she'd wickedly done to those she felt had wronged her in some way, she failed to see Ava trying to get Stackz's gun on the sly.

"Leela," her mother had finally come to and was delirious, stumbling down the hallway.

Seeing that her sister was momentarily distracted, Ava made one last-ditch effort to get Stackz's gun but was caught.

"Naw, bitch, naw! I know you don't think you that slick, or is it you think I'm that stupid? Either/or, all three of y'all motherfuckers gonna die tonight!" Leela raised her gun once more, aiming it directly at Ava's face.

Before Leela could pull the trigger, a thunderous sound of one single shot rang out, echoing off the walls. The ear-deafening blast went in through her lower back, causing her to fall to her knees. Leela's face was full of anguish. It told the agonizing story of pain, betrayal, hate, and low self-esteem in its purest form. As Leela gave in to death, she slumped over to the side. Behind Leela, her oldest daughter was in tears, having been knocked clear across the room after firing her grandmother's old-school .410 sawed off shotgun she'd been constantly warned to never touch unless it was an emergency.

Ava couldn't believe what had just happened. She was frozen until the annoying alert tone of her sister's cell snapped her out of her dazed trance. After calling the ambulance for Stackz, her mother, and herself from her cell, she took Leela's phone out of her back pocket. Reading the text Rank had just sent, Ava now had the address of where he wanted her sister to meet up with him. Wanting to put an end to all of her and Stackz's problems, Ava called T. L., telling him what had just happened and where he could catch up with an unsuspecting Rank. After tonight, there would be no loose ends. She and Stackz could finally be free to live their lives in peace.

THE END